Only Fiona

Only Fiona
by Beverly Keller

A Harper Trophy Book
Harper & Row, Publishers

Library of Congress Cataloging-in-Publication Data
Keller, Beverly.
  Only Fiona.

  Summary: Despite several comic mishaps, ten-year-
old Fiona's campaign to convince those around her of
the importance of being humane to animals brings her
respect and new friends.
  [1. Animals—Treatment—Fiction. 2. Friendship—
Fiction. 3. Humorous stories] I. Title.
PZ7.K2813On 1988   [Fic]   86-45786
ISBN 0-06-023269-2
ISBN 0-06-023270-6 (lib. bdg.).
ISBN 0-06-440290-8 (pbk.)

First Harper Trophy edition, 1989.

For Christopher Werby

Only Fiona

1

"It's better never to be famous than to be famous for just a few days," Fiona Foster told her mother while they cleaned up after breakfast.

Mrs. Foster brushed off the place mats. "I wouldn't know."

"I was famous when we first moved here." Fiona stacked the dishes and saucers and cups and carried them over to the dishwasher. It was always interesting—and a little scary—to see how many breakable things she could carry in one trip. Her parents seemed to trust her to not make too wobbly a pile, but she could not help imagining the terrible and exciting mess there would be if things weren't balanced quite right.

"Anybody can be famous with other kids just by

being new in town." Fiona set the cups and saucers and dishes on the counter beside her father. "But does it last? No! In a day or two, it's all over."

"There are drawbacks to being famous," her father observed.

"I didn't notice any." Fiona watched him stick the knives and forks and spoons into the dishwasher basket every which way.

"Truly famous people can't go anywhere without being pestered for autographs," he reminded her.

"I could live with it," Fiona said.

Mrs. Foster carried the syrup and margarine to the refrigerator. "Don't put the knives in the dishwasher with the points up," she reminded her husband, without even looking to see if that was what he was doing.

The house they'd lived in before had had no dishwasher. It had had only one bathroom, and a small, scrubby backyard. Six weeks had passed since they had moved out of that house, and Fiona still thought of it as home.

The house they lived in now had two stories, two bathrooms, and a yard with a big patio and plenty of room for a swing set. The only thing wrong with the new house was that it felt like a new house.

She knew there were very good reasons for moving from Kelsey, where she'd lived all her life, to Elvern.

"A job offer like this doesn't come every day," her mother had told her solemnly. "Elvern is ten times bigger than Kelsey, and Molberry's Department Store there is in a brand-new shopping mall, and your father will be manager of the entire optical department."

"It will be a real opportunity for your mother," Mr. Foster had told Fiona earnestly. "There's no future for a computer programmer in a town where the biggest business is Kelsey Lumber and Hardware. This way, she'll be in contact with up-and-coming firms that understand about computers."

Against all these good and serious reasons, what argument did Fiona have? Only "I don't want to go." She had said it a couple of times, just as solemnly and earnestly, but it had only set off a new round of sincere explanations from her parents. Finally she had given up, realizing they were going to move no matter what.

In the six weeks they'd lived in Elvern, Fiona had seen enough of it to realize it was a much handsomer town than Kelsey. Just a few blocks from Fiona's new house was a huge park. Its trees were so tall and leafy, they seemed to be whispering even when there was no breeze. There were acres of fine, close-trimmed grass, with gentle mounds you could roll down if you took a notion.

Molberry's Department Store was the biggest store Fiona had ever seen, set in the middle of a shopping mall that was nearly as dazzling as Disneyland. Molberry's Optical Department had brand-new carpeting and chairs and *four* glass-topped tables with mirrors where customers could sit and try on frames.

The only thing wrong with Elvern, Fiona thought, is that it feels like a new town, too.

"The hardest thing about leaving a place," she told her mother now, "is giving up your friends. I knew most of those kids in Kelsey so long, I couldn't even remember how I met them. The neat thing about friends like that is that you can just count on them. You know. Not for anything special. Just to be around." She started wiping down the counter. "You don't even care about being famous when you have friends to count on."

"You've made new friends since we moved here," her mother reminded her gently.

"Not to count on. Besides, they all live blocks away." Fiona set the sponge beside the sink. "To learn to live in a new place, you have to have a brother or a sister or a dog or a cat going through it with you, or friends you can count on."

No sooner had she gotten the last word out than Fiona realized she hadn't included parents among the things she could count on. Not only that, the things she *had* mentioned, like brothers and sisters, were mostly things parents provide. In one sentence, she thought, I insulted my mother and father in at least two different ways.

"I think it's my personality," she said hastily, to let them know she didn't blame them. "There's something about me that makes people take me for granted. Look at the kids I've met in Elvern. The only time

6

Pauline comes looking for me is when she can't find Barbara. The only time Barbara comes over is when she's looking for Pauline. When Howard went to the beach, he left his dog with me because Spike gets carsick. Then he took Larry."

Mr. Foster glanced helplessly at Mrs. Foster.

Mrs. Foster put her arms around Fiona, getting a smear of syrup on her neck. "You're having a bad day, aren't you, love?"

"It's only morning," Fiona pointed out.

"Things are bound to get better," her father assured her. "It takes a while to settle in, but once you get used to Elvern, you'll be glad we moved here."

Fiona had a feeling that if she asked "Why?" or "When?" she would get no more-definite answers, so she only nodded. There was no point depressing her parents, and herself, any more than she had already.

As soon as the kitchen was tidied, she went out on the front porch.

It was a lovely, lazy Saturday morning, warm enough already for running through the sprinklers, if you had anybody to run through the sprinklers with. Fiona could imagine nothing more embarrassing than being seen running through a sprinkler all by yourself.

Across the street, a man was trimming his front hedge with electric clippers. Next door to him a woman was mowing her front lawn with an electric mower.

One thing about a nice neighborhood, Fiona thought, the people certainly take care of their yards. They certainly have the machinery to do it with, too.

At least the Fourth of July had been over for a week, so there was no need to go around tensed for stray firecracker explosions.

Fiona picked up her red dog dish and carried it down to the faucet under the living room window. Even before she'd moved to Elvern, she had longed for a dog, or a cat, or even a rat—more than a brother or sister, in fact. Some of her friends in Kelsey had had brothers and sisters. Some had had pets. Fiona could not help noticing the difference: Animals didn't need diaper changing, or have tantrums, or try to grab all the good shades of crayons.

It was definitely a handicap to have parents who were allergic to dog hair, cat hair, and feathers—and who weren't too crazy about rats.

With her first allowance after moving to Elvern, Fiona had bought a dog dish. "Sweetheart," her mother had said patiently, but looking a little worried, "this is no way to try to pressure us into getting a dog."

"I know," Fiona had told her. "But a dog dish is a sensible thing to put outside in summer. People have birdbaths, but hardly anybody worries about dogs and cats out on the streets in hot weather."

So far, no dog or cat had dropped by for a drink, but a bee had dropped into the dish. Fiona had had a tense and scary time fishing it out of the dish and taking it to a safe place to dry off.

8

Since then, she'd left the dog dish empty when she wasn't around to watch it.

As Fiona was filling the dish, Barbara Lawson tromped up the walk, pushing her little brother, Oliver, in his stroller.

Almost eleven, Barbara was a few months older than Fiona, and half a head taller. Her hair was a darker brown than Fiona's, and cut shorter, and her eyes were a light brown flecked with bits of gold. She was square built but not bulky. Fiona could imagine her growing up to be a general, or maybe a wrestler. Barbara did not look like a person who backed down easily.

She was also the first genuine child grump Fiona had ever met. Back in Kelsey there were a few grown-ups who were generally known to be grumps—everybody avoided cutting across their front yards, or cut across on purpose just to get a reaction.

A child grump, though, was something Fiona had never run into before. She had known kids who were irritable now and then, but Barbara was just grumpy by nature, grumpy at everybody, and grumpy for no particular reason. Fiona couldn't help wondering whether Barbara had been born that way, or whether she had grown into it. She pictured a newborn Barbara, squalling in her cradle, glaring at the world.

If there was a naturally cranky strain running in Barbara's family, her little brother, Oliver, did not seem to have caught it.

9

Every time Fiona had seen him so far, he'd been in his stroller. Oliver seemed to take things as they came. He looked to be somewhere between one and two years old; Fiona had never bothered to ask, since he didn't do anything very interesting.

His hair was blond and soft and curly, his gaze was innocent and gentle, and he didn't talk, which made him almost as agreeable to be around as a dog.

As a matter of fact, Oliver seemed to have more in common with the average dog than with his sister. He took an interest in things that any human over the age of two generally overlooked. He peered at everything he passed in his stroller, and tried to smell and taste anything he got his hands on. He fussed hard, but not long, when his sister grabbed leaves or tree bark or old gum wrappers as he was about to eat them.

Barbara stomped up Fiona's walk now. Even when she was in a relatively good mood, Barbara tended to walk as if she were punishing the sidewalk on general principles.

"Nobody's home at Pauline's," she greeted Fiona. "I wonder where she went."

Fiona carried the dog dish up to the porch. What would happen, she wondered, if I just came right out and said, "Do you know you never come around here unless you're looking for Pauline?"

"Do you remember her saying anything about where she was going?" Barbara stood with her hands on the stroller handle, ready to take off the minute she knew where Pauline was.

Before Fiona could answer, she saw Howard Broyhill crossing the street with his dog, Spike.

Howard was barely ten, but taller than Barbara. His skin was the color of chocolate, and his hair was black and crisp and curly. Fiona had never seen him without Spike, who looked like a sheepdog mixed with an assortment of other breeds. Spike's back legs were longer than his front legs, so he walked rather like a bear. His hair was long, gray and white, and shaggy, even on his head—Fiona had never been able to get a good look at his eyes.

Howard patted Oliver on the head absently, as he would a dog, and told Fiona and Barbara, "My folks are taking me—"

Fiona set down the dog dish. "And you want me to watch Spike."

Howard looked surprised. "No. We won't be gone that long. My folks said I could bring a couple of friends. You guys want to come—without Oliver?"

Spike plopped his front right paw in the dog dish, sloshing water over the porch. Fiona barely noticed. This was the first time anyone in Elvern had asked her to go anywhere. "Yeah! Sure! Great!"

"Where?" Barbara asked.

"To the zoo."

Fiona's delight fizzed away like the bubbles from a

11

soda that's been left out all day. The whole idea of zoos made her sad. "No, thanks."

"What's the matter?" Howard asked.

"I've been to the zoo." Fiona just wanted to go inside and be left alone to feel disappointed in private.

"There's some law against going twice?" Barbara wanted to know. Barbara often asked questions that were like statements. Fiona suspected it was because they sounded grumpier that way.

"A minute ago you were all excited," Howard reminded Fiona.

"It's the animals," she explained.

"That's why you *go* to the zoo." Barbara spoke as if she were explaining to a visitor from another planet. "You *go* to look at the animals."

"Cooped up in cages?" Fiona could see she was upsetting Howard and Barbara, but she felt she owed it to the zoo animals to speak out.

"You want them walking the streets?" Barbara demanded. "Riding the bus? Shopping in the mall?"

Though Fiona was impressed that Barbara could fire three sentence-questions in a row, she was not even tempted to back down. "They should be where they can do what they feel like doing, and not just hang around being watched," she said firmly.

"Hey, they have a good time!" But Howard was beginning to sound as if he were trying to convince himself. "Didn't you ever see the bears beg for peanuts?"

"Would you sit up and grab your feet and rock back and forth for a crummy peanut?" Fiona asked.

"Okay. That's it. Forget it." Barbara whirled Oliver's stroller around. "Nobody can talk to her."

Fiona sat on her porch steps, watching Howard and Barbara walk away with Oliver. Spike followed them, sniffing at bugs and twigs, and catching his leash under his front leg.

Even knowing Barbara was a grump didn't make Fiona feel better. Here it is, barely after breakfast, she thought, and I've already insulted my parents and Barbara and Howard, the only person in this town who's ever invited me anyplace. And he came to my house first, not Barbara's.

The idea hit her, *whop!*, just like that.

"Hey!" She leaped to her feet and ran after Howard and Barbara.

They stopped while she caught up.

"You might as well leave Spike with me," she said, trying to sound casual and offhand.

"Great!" One neat thing about Howard, he didn't cherish a grudge. He handed Spike's leash to Fiona. "He'll be a lot happier with a person than with a chew toy." Howard bent to kiss the bit of wet black nose that showed through Spike's hair.

"We'll dump Oliver at my house first," Barbara told Howard, as if Fiona hadn't done anything noble or generous at all.

13

"You're sure you don't mind leaving him?" Howard asked.

"Do you think I'd go for a long ride with anybody who wears diapers?" Barbara started walking again, pushing the stroller.

And that was it. Not so much as "Wow, Fiona, what a big favor." Not even "You must really love dogs, Fiona."

As Howard caught up to her, Barbara asked, "Who else shall we get to come with us?"

"I don't know," Fiona heard him say. "Everybody else either isn't home or has something to do."

A person can be too offhand and casual, Fiona reflected.

She led Spike back to her house. It was only half a block, but it took time. Since he walked with his face inches from the ground he noticed a lot of things the average person overlooks. Every few steps he stopped to sniff, and lick, and nudge things with his nose.

Fiona reached her front yard as her mother came out the door.

"Oh, Fiona." Mrs. Foster looked surprised. "You were just complaining about watching that dog."

Fiona didn't answer. The dog, she thought, is the only person so far this morning who hasn't told me I'm just having a bad day, or that nobody can talk to me.

Mrs. Foster hurried toward the station wagon. Your mother may make mistakes sometimes, like giving you slapdash comfort when you need serious sympathy,

14

but there's no sense doing yourself out of a ride that could end with a stop for a banana split. Fiona went after her. "Where are you going?"

Mrs. Foster unlocked the door of the old blue station wagon. "Just to pick up some spray. We've got ants coming in under the kitchen sink."

Fiona pulled Spike back as he tried to crowd into the wagon. "You're going to spray them before you even find out what they plan to do?"

"Fiona, I am really not prepared to argue about ants' plans."

Fiona could see that her mother was in no mood to discuss the matter.

"You've probably never watched ants enough to think about them," Fiona said. "Ants are neat, when you get to know them."

Mrs. Foster slid into the car.

Spike planted his front paws on the hood, barking urgently.

Looking a little strained, Mrs. Foster waited for Fiona to haul Spike down on all fours. Then she put the key in the ignition. "Try to keep him quiet, honey. The last time he stayed here, he howled and yapped and drove us half crazy."

"But he settled down."

"He lay on his back on our porch with his legs stiff in the air. The neighbors probably thought we'd taken up taxidermy."

"Tax . . . like in taxes or taxis?"

"Taxidermy." Mrs. Foster turned the key. "Stuffing dead animals so they look almost alive. I guess you never saw the moose head on the wall of the sporting goods department at Kelsey Lumber and Hardware."

Fiona stood back from the car. "Mother! That is *gross!*"

"Indeed. So keep Spike quiet, and off his back." Mrs. Foster drove away.

The station wagon's paint had gone dull, and even the license plates were dented and old. In any other family where both parents earned money, Fiona thought, there would be two cars, or at least one that looked respectable.

"But that's the way my folks are." She led Spike back up the porch steps and sat down. "My dad spends half his day fitting contact lenses, but he wears glasses. My mom works all day at her computer with *her* glasses sliding down her nose, so she has to shove them back every two minutes."

It occurred to her that Spike probably hadn't seen his own mother since he was a few weeks old. The idea made her so sad, she had to grumble a little just to keep from feeling more downcast.

"When your own mother doesn't even ask if you want to come to the store," she told Spike, "that shows how much she thinks of you. Sure, she'd say it was because certain dogs around here have a reputation for getting carsick. Sure, I wouldn't go—that would be like approving of ant spray. But she could have at least asked."

Spike slumped against Fiona so she had to brace herself.

"Sure, Barbara says nobody can talk to me," Fiona went on, "but what does everybody talk to me *about*? About animals locked up in zoos. About moose heads on walls. About murdering ants. I mean, these ants wander in under the sink, right? Were there any *Keep Out* signs to warn them? They're not planning to steal our TV, after all. Maybe they're looking for something to eat. Maybe they're *starving*. Since when is that a crime? Maybe they're just going to take a look around and then get out of there. But right away, *zap!*, they're massacred."

Spike twisted his head around to chew at imaginary fleas on his shoulder.

So long as she was resenting things, Fiona told him about the time she got in trouble for accidentally scuffing her new patent-leather shoes. Then she told him how she got blamed when she was five for biting her cousin Ethel, even though Ethel had pinched her first.

Spike snored a soft, wet-sounding snore.

Fiona tied his leash to the porch rail and went into the house to try to reason with her father.

He was squatting beside the dishwasher, taking cleaners and detergents and scouring pads from the cabinet under the sink.

17

Gazing around the kitchen, Fiona said, "I see they haven't taken over or anything."

He took out a bottle of plant fertilizer and a roll of paper towels. "Who?"

"The ants."

Mr. Foster ripped a few sheets of towel off the roll. "They're enough to drive you crazy."

"It's not like having rattlesnakes or scorpions in your kitchen," Fiona said reasonably.

He reached back with the paper towels. "Will you dampen these, honey?"

Fiona ran the towels under the faucet and squeezed them out. "The ants might just be passing through." She handed him the wet towels. "Why is it the first thing people think of when they see anything *really* little is to squash it or spray it?"

Mrs. Foster came in the back door. "Fiona, that dog is lying on his back on our front porch, looking like a large dead bug. And if he comes to life and jumps on the mail carrier, we could be sued." Setting a sack on the counter, she took out a can of spray.

"Since there's nothing to eat under the sink, maybe the ants will get discouraged and leave," Fiona said.

"Why don't we have sandwiches for lunch?" Mrs. Foster asked her husband. "Then we won't have to wash dishes before we spray."

"If we give them a couple of days to leave on their own," Fiona argued, "they might never come back."

Her mother opened a loaf of bread, and her father started taking jars out of the refrigerator.

"Fiona, would you move the dog, and get the dish of water off the steps before somebody steps in it?" Mrs. Foster fished in the pickle jar with a fork.

"You're going to do it, aren't you?" Fiona asked flatly. "You're just going to go ahead and do it, no matter what I say!"

Mr. Foster put his hand on Fiona's cheek and looked down at her sincerely. "Honey, we don't want you to feel bad, but we can't just turn over the house to an ant colony. Now, you go do what your mother asked."

"My parents take me for granted. Even *dogs* take me for granted." Fiona trudged out of the kitchen.

"Poor lamb," she heard her mother murmur. "She *is* in a mood today."

As Fiona came out the front door, Spike clambered to his feet, wagging as if he'd been left alone for weeks. He looked like a haystack in a hurricane, especially since he wagged his whole body, and shed as he wagged.

Fiona untied his leash and led him through the gate to the side yard. After she looped the end of his leash over the knob of the garage door, she went back through the gate to fetch the water dish.

She set it far enough from Spike so he couldn't step in it, then went around to the back door.

On the kitchen table were paper plates and cups

19

and napkins. Even the sandwiches and fruit and pound cake were on paper plates.

Fiona picked up a sandwich and started to peel back the bread.

"*Don't* open it," her mother said. "It's chopped olive."

Fiona piled sandwiches and cake on a paper plate. "I guess I'll eat outside, so I won't have to think about the ants being slaughtered."

"*Good*," her father said.

"Wait a minute," Mrs. Foster said, as Fiona headed for the door. "You are not to feed chopped olives and pound cake to that dog."

Fiona began putting the sandwiches back slowly, half by half.

With a sigh, Mrs. Foster handed her two other sandwich halves. "That is all he gets. And he'll have to settle for peanut butter." Then she took all but one slice of pound cake off Fiona's plate.

Fiona took time to put an apple in her mouth before she picked up the plate and a cup of lemonade.

With an apple in her mouth and her hands full and Spike leaping up to greet her, she had to move very, very carefully.

Sitting down a few feet from him, her back against the garage wall, she tossed him half a sandwich.

He gulped it, then sat with his eyes fixed on her plate.

"Boy," she muttered. "Nobody can stare at food the way a dog can." She tossed him the second half of a peanut butter sandwich. "Don't try to make me feel guilty. If you chewed like a normal person, you wouldn't finish so fast."

He watched her eat.

After half a chopped-olive sandwich, she gave up. "Okay." She tossed him the other half sandwich. "Here's the deal. The pound cake is all mine. Howard wouldn't want you to eat it anyway. It's full of sugar."

She turned her back to Spike, and saw what she hadn't noticed when she had been navigating with her hands and mouth full.

A line of ants stretched from the bushes by the fence, across the walk, and into the flower bed under the bathroom window.

Fiona heard the back door open. "I'll spray around the foundation of the house," she heard her father say, "so they don't find another way in."

Fiona leaped to her feet, scattering crumbs.

2

There is no way to move a line of ants. There is no way to hide a line of ants, or to reason with a line of ants.

Fiona heard the hiss of the spray can.

Spike got to his feet, growling under his breath.

Mr. Foster came around the corner of the house, aiming the spray at the foundation.

"Wait!" Fiona stepped between her father and the ants.

"Move, honey." Her father aimed the nozzle at the wall by his feet and pressed the button.

Barking savagely, straining at the leash, Spike sprang forward.

"What . . ." Mr. Foster pulled Fiona back. "Stay clear!"

"It's the spray can!" Fiona told him. "Spike must think it's a short fat snake."

Spike snarled, his hackles up.

"Burt, you have a phone call from the store. It's some kind of emergency." Mrs. Foster came around the side of the house.

Mr. Foster handed the can to her. "Don't get near that animal!" He hurried around to the back door.

Mrs. Foster ignored Spike, who was wagging like a dust mop being shaken. "I don't know why the store has to have a crisis on your father's day off. Where did he stop spraying?"

"Ma'am?" Fiona tried to look puzzled.

Mr. Foster opened the bathroom window. "I have to run back to the store. The sprinkler system has flooded the optical department and the sprinkler company's answering machine doesn't work. Where are my shoes?"

"Where did you stop spraying?" Mrs. Foster asked him.

"About where you're standing. I can't go to the store in rubber thongs, Mae."

Thongs seemed like sensible footgear to wear to a flood, Fiona thought, but she knew this was no time to say so.

"Look under the bed." Mrs. Foster aimed the spray can at the foundation of the house.

At the first hiss Spike leaped forward, snarling and barking.

"What in the world . . ." Mrs. Foster thrust Fiona behind her.

"Back!" Mr. Foster shouted at Spike through the screen. "Back, I say!"

"Spike's protecting you!" Fiona told her mother. "He thinks the can's attacking you. See? As soon as you stop spraying, he wags his tail."

"That dog's a killer!" Mr. Foster yelled through the window.

"Oh, don't be silly, Burt," Mrs. Foster said. "It *is* the spray can."

"You stay out of his reach anyway," Mr. Foster called to Fiona. "Where under the bed?"

"Wherever you left them," Mrs. Foster said, but she set the spray can on the chimney ledge and walked around to the back door.

Fiona went after her. "Shall I throw away the spray can?" she asked hopefully.

"Don't you touch it!" her mother said firmly. "I'll finish up after the dog's gone."

In all the furor, Fiona's parents hadn't even noticed the line of ants. "But they'll be back," she told Spike. "You won't be here to hold them off forever."

She squatted a few inches clear of him and watched the ants.

They'd discovered a few of the pound cake crumbs on the walk. Two or three were working at each crumb, pushing and hauling, even trying to lift it. Other ants

24

were running back along the line, rubbing feelers with the newcomers excitedly, as if to say, "Hey, guys! You won't believe this! Wait until you see what dropped out of *nowhere*!"

"Look at them," Fiona told Spike. "So happy. So thrilled. No suspicion that they're going to be wiped out."

As she watched, an idea gathered itself together in her mind. The ants were trying to move the crumbs *away* from the house. Carefully, she crawled back along the ant trail, under the scraggly bushes in the side yard. There, by the side fence, was a big sandy anthill.

Fiona heard the station wagon depart.

She hurried around the back of the house to the kitchen.

She could hear her mother working on the computer in her office.

There was no pound cake left. Fiona spooned a little white sugar into a paper cup. It's probably no better for ants than it is for people, she thought, but it beats being sprayed. Then she made up little foil packets of peanut butter, honey, and granola, and put them in the cup.

Fiona hurried out. There was no sense interrupting her mother to explain. There was no point in calling her mother's *attention* to the ants.

As soon as he saw Fiona coming around the house, Spike began yelping and dancing.

More ants were trying to move more pound cake crumbs.

As Fiona crawled under the bushes with the paper cup in her teeth, Spike was suddenly silent, fascinated.

Several inches from the anthill, Fiona sat back on her heels.

There was no time for anything fancy. She scraped peanut butter and honey off the foil, then off her fingers. She dumped granola into a separate little pile. Then she emptied the sugar.

As she backed out from under the bushes, Spike bounded to greet her. She heard something clank on the walk. Then she saw the knob of the garage door roll across the concrete.

Before she could get to her feet, Spike gamboled toward her.

"*No!*" she cried.

His right front paw landed in the water dish.

As the dish tipped, water swept over the pound cake crumbs and the ants on the walk.

"Fiona?" she heard her mother call.

"I'm all right!" she shouted. "I'm fine! No problem!"

Some of the ants had been swept right off the walk. Some struggled to regain their footing. Some wandered, dazed and aimless. Already, the soaked pound cake crumbs were dissolving.

Fiona knew that anybody who'd been a mother for ten years would not rely on her child's assurance that she'd yelled "No!" without a reason. Fiona knew that if her mother came around the house and saw the ants, she'd simply turn the hose on them and wash them off the walk.

There was also the matter of the garage doorknob.

Fiona dropped to her hands and knees and blew gently on the ants, whooshing them off the walk toward the bushes.

Having been a child for ten years, Fiona knew a pulled-out doorknob called for a prompt confession. She picked up the knob and the soggy paper plate. Holding Spike's leash firmly, she led him around the back of the house.

Spike was in no hurry. He had to smell the flowers and wet on the bushes and eat a little grass and throw it up and jump back in alarm from a caterpillar.

Mrs. Foster was opening the back door as Fiona reached it.

"Why is it suddenly so quiet?" she asked. "Didn't your father tell you to stay clear of that dog? And what's that in your hand?"

Fiona held out her hand. "When the knob came off the garage door, the leash came off the knob."

Spike sat back on his haunches and lifted his front paws, like a bear begging for peanuts.

Mrs. Foster backed into a kitchen chair, sat, and put her head in her hands.

"Mama?" Looping the leash around the railing, Fiona hurried into the kitchen. "Mama, are you laughing or crying?"

"I haven't decided." Mrs. Foster rested her elbows on the kitchen table and her chin on her left palm. "Do I blame the dog, or the person who attached his leash to the knob, or her parents for not telling her to take the leash off the knob?" She stood. "I hate to ignore you on a Saturday, Fiona, but I've got a deadline. Just keep the dog in the backyard and don't let him do any more damage."

Fiona led Spike back to the side yard. "We're just lucky she feels guilty about working when I'm around," she told him.

There was not an ant on the walk. Those in the dirt near it were milling around in confusion. Gripping the leash close to Spike's collar, Fiona crawled under the bushes.

The ants had discovered the food she'd left. A few were investigating the honey and peanut butter and granola. The biggest crowd was gathered around the white sugar.

Suddenly, Spike yelped. Tearing the leash from Fiona's hand, he scrambled out from under the bushes.

Fiona had no idea whether he'd been attacked by ants or was having a fit. "It's okay! It's okay!" Hastily, she backed out from under the bushes.

"Hey, boy!"

Spike was on his hind legs, frantically licking Howard's face.

"What are you doing under the bushes?" Barbara asked Fiona.

Fiona stood. "Watching ants."

"*Ants?*" Barbara echoed. "You turn down a trip to the zoo to watch *ants*? We saw lions, and giraffes, and bears, and hippos—"

"Doing what?" Fiona asked.

"What do you mean, doing what?" Barbara asked. "You expect them to be writing poetry or something?"

"I mean, what were they doing?"

"Not much." Howard rubbed his cheek against Spike's muzzle.

"At least it beats watching ants," Barbara said loftily.

"I don't suppose you know that ants have great table manners," Fiona said, "even though they're junk food freaks."

"Come on!" Barbara scoffed.

"I'll show you." Fiona crawled back under the bushes. "Hang on to Spike."

A few inches from the anthill, she sat back on her heels. "See? Right to the sugar."

Even Barbara was impressed. "Wow! Maybe that's why ants are so small."

Fiona and Howard looked at her.

"They're so polite." Howard leaned his elbows on his knees. "All those ants around one pile of sugar without any of them crowding or shoving."

"And look," Fiona said. "They space themselves evenly, like tiny spokes around the center of a wheel."

"I like those guys who already found the sugar rushing around to tell the ones just coming from the nest," Howard said.

"A few of them are tasting . . . what's that stuff?" Barbara asked.

"Honey, and granola, and peanut butter."

"I feel sorry for the ones trying to tell everybody about the granola," Howard said.

Fiona heard her family station wagon pull into the driveway. "Quick! Back out! Get away from the ants!"

"Why? Why?" Howard and Barbara whispered, but they obeyed.

Fiona urged them out the side gate. "Get Spike away from here!"

She went in through the garage and met her father in the driveway. "Hi, Dad." She tried to think of something that would keep his mind off the ants. "How was your flood?"

"Mmmfth." He trudged up the porch steps. She could tell by his slouch that it would be some time before he'd feel up to spraying anything.

She caught up to Howard and Barbara and Spike at the corner.

"Why did we have to get away from the side yard?" Barbara asked. "And why did we have to get Spike away?"

"I like having him around, since he won't let anybody kill the ants. But when my father sees where he pulled the knob off the door . . ."

"Wait. Wait." Howard stopped walking. "Spike won't let anybody hurt ants?"

Fiona explained about Spike attacking the spray can.

"Wow!" Kneeling, Howard put his arms around Spike. "Just like Lassie!"

"It was a spray can, not a rattler," Barbara pointed out.

Howard looked up at her coldly. "My *dog* didn't know that."

They walked on to the park. Fiona told them about the ants trying to carry crumbs away from the house, about trying to coax them back to their hill, Spike flooding them, her blowing them off the walk, and Spike pulling the knob off the door.

When she finished, Howard said, "Is it okay if we come over tomorrow to see what's happening?"

"It won't be easy," Fiona said. "So long as I can feed the ants and keep them under the bushes, they're safe. But we can't call attention to them."

Barbara raised her eyebrows. "Your parents are going to crawl under bushes looking for them?"

"No," Fiona said patiently. "But if we're hanging around there all the time, they're going to wonder why."

"One of us can stand watch," Howard suggested. "If I even hear a door open, I'll warn you. It'll be exciting. . . ."

31

"How come *we* go to the zoo, and everything exciting happens to *you*?" Barbara asked Fiona. "We don't even *get* ants around our house."

"Sure you do," Howard said. "You probably just don't notice unless they get in and everybody starts making a fuss."

This was what Fiona had been trying not to think about. "I couldn't save the ones in the house," she murmured.

Howard stopped and faced her and put his hands on her shoulders. "Hey. Fiona. How many people do you know who could have saved *any* ants? What would happen to those ants in the yard if they didn't have you to count on?"

When Fiona got home, she didn't go back to the kitchen for a snack. She was afraid it would still smell of ant spray.

Hearing the *click click click* of computer keys, she wandered into her mother's office. Mrs. Foster sat squinting at the monitor, her glasses sliding down her nose.

Fiona felt as if somebody put a hand around her heart and squeezed, not hard but tight. I love them so much it hurts sometimes, she thought. They spray ants without even thinking about it. But that's the way they were brought up.

Mrs. Foster swiveled around in her chair. She looked

tired and rumpled, but she smiled and put her arms out. "Hi, sweetie!"

Fiona hugged her, wondering what would happen if she told her mother the whole story.

"Want something to eat?" her mother asked, still holding her.

"Could we have it out on the porch?"

Fiona went into the downstairs bathroom and washed her hands. When she came out, her mother was sitting on the front-porch swing with two bananas and a box of English tea biscuits.

Fiona sat on the swing, peeling the banana her mother had started for her. It was almost four o'clock, the time when the heat of a July day shimmers off the sidewalks, and people go inside—unless they're running through sprinklers with their friends. The street was so quiet, you could hear the murmuring of bugs.

"You're right about being famous." Fiona took a tea biscuit out of the box. "It could be a pain." She remembered what Howard had said. "You know what does feel good, though? What feels really good is being somebody to count on."

"You are one smart kid," her mother said.

It also feels good to be appreciated, Fiona thought. But she was sure any mother already knew that.

3

August was a lonely time for Fiona. Howard and his family and Spike went to Yellowstone Park. Larry's mother sent him to spend the month with his father. Barbara and Pauline went to summer camp.

Even the ants moved. One afternoon they were all busy around the anthill. The next morning it was deserted.

Fiona worried that it was because of her. Maybe they'd gotten sick of the same old food. Maybe they'd gotten tired of being watched, although they'd never given any sign they knew she was watching them. She always figured that she was too enormous for them to take in, just as she'd have no idea if something bigger than all the planets were watching her.

The thought scared her more than lying on her back and staring into the sky.

She told herself the ants had just moved on, the same way her parents had moved to Elvern.

Finally, it was the middle of August and Barbara and Pauline came back.

"I missed them while they were at camp," Fiona told her mother.

Mrs. Foster glanced up from her computer monitor. "It must be nice to have them around again."

Fiona thought for a minute. "I think I liked them better when they were away, though. Now that they're back, all they talk about is camp, and the counselors, and the sing-alongs, and the animals. They call all the staff by nicknames, so I can't tell whether they're talking about a person or a horse."

Mrs. Foster turned her chair around to face Fiona. "Honey, you should have told us you wanted to go to camp with them."

Fiona was amazed sometimes by the things her mother didn't know. "Mama, they've been going there together for three summers. You don't just go to camp at the same time unless they *ask* you to."

"Maybe it never occurred to them." Mrs. Foster leaned forward to cup Fiona's face in her hands. "You have to learn to be more assertive."

"Assertive? What does that mean?"

"You have to speak up and tell people how you feel. You have to go after what you want, and not sit around and wait to be invited."

"Are you and Dad assertive?"

Mrs. Foster turned back to her keyboard. "We're going to take a class in assertiveness, as soon as we get the time."

Fiona wondered if she would have to take a class to be assertive. I'd better not ask, she decided. With Mama feeling sorry about my missing camp, I could find myself signed up this very day. Besides, I could learn how to be assertive just from watching Barbara.

A few days later, Pauline came down with stomach flu, and Barbara stopped talking about camp.

Instead, she talked about her sister's wedding.

"My mother was going to have the downstairs painted, but my father threw a fit." Barbara lounged on her back lawn, with Fiona sprawled on one side of her and Oliver in his stroller at the other. "He said we weren't going to pay to have the parlor painted when we're renting a tent."

Fiona sat up, fascinated. "Your family's going to move into a tent just to pay for a wedding?"

"Not to *live* in. Not the camping kind." Barbara sounded like a teacher trying to keep her patience. "A big party tent, with no sides." She grabbed for Oliver as he clambered out of his stroller. He'd just learned to climb out, but he hadn't got the knack of doing it without falling on his head.

Fiona was puzzled.

"No sides?"

"You think two hundred people could mingle around in a tent with sides? You think this is the Superdome or something?" Barbara's voice was sharp as she plopped Oliver down on the grass.

"Two hundred people?" Fiona couldn't imagine even knowing two hundred people.

Barbara nodded, calmed by Fiona's respect. "We sent out over two hundred invitations. There'll be long tables under the tent, with every kind of food you can imagine, and two kinds of punch, and a three-tier wedding cake. Nobody sits down, of course. They walk around the tables and eat and drink."

As Barbara talked on, Fiona gazed across the backyard. The size of four Foster yards, it was so neat there was no hint that children ever played in it. The hedges were twice Fiona's height, glossy and perfectly trimmed. The grass was smooth and green, without a single tan patch.

Fiona imagined an enormous tent in the middle of the lawn, looking like a hot-air balloon flattened out, held up by gilded poles. They'd be the twisted kind that carousels had on the horses that went up and down. She pictured long tables piled with ribbon sandwiches and mixed nuts and green and pink and yellow mints. There would be men in ice-cream-colored suits and women in dresses as soft and bright as butterfly wings strolling around, sipping ruby-colored punch from clear glass cups.

Since the Lawsons didn't even know the Fosters, Fiona realized there was no chance she would see this wedding.

"And we're hiring a three-piece orchestra," Barbara was saying.

Two hundred people, Fiona thought. Out of two hundred people, there was a chance two or three wouldn't be able to come. With only a couple of days now until the wedding, the Lawsons might be trying to figure out whom they could invite on such short notice. At any minute Mrs. Lawson might glance out the window and say, "Wait. There's Barbara's little friend, Fiona. See how she puts up with Oliver? Her family's new in town, too. Wouldn't it be a nice touch to include them in the wedding?"

Oliver gagged.

"He's eating grass," Fiona told Barbara.

"He always does." Prying Oliver's mouth open, Barbara stuck in her thumb and finger. *"Spit it out!"* She pulled out a few blades of chewed grass an instant before Oliver clamped his teeth together. Before he could get himself collected and start kicking, she stuck him back in his stroller.

"My sister's veil is six feet long." Barbara wiped the

chewed grass on her jeans. "But I'll be walking ahead of her."

"Ahead of her?"

Rolling her eyes at Fiona's ignorance, Barbara clapped her hand on Oliver's shoulder to hold him in his stroller. "Of course. I'm a *flower* girl. Flower girls walk in front of the bride carrying little baskets of flowers."

"Why?"

"Fiona Foster, you don't know anything about anything!" Leaping to her feet, Barbara spun the stroller around and stalked toward her back door.

Grumps just don't have the patience to do much explaining, Fiona thought, feeling a little cranky herself. The only thing to do is go home and forget about the wedding.

It is not easy to forget about a party to which you're not invited. Fiona kept thinking about Barbara, in a flower-girl dress, walking ahead of her sister, with people who didn't actually *know* Barbara whispering, "Isn't she adorable?"

Setting the table for dinner, Fiona couldn't help but think of the wedding tables. At bedtime, even though she knew she was being dumb, she got out her best dress to make sure it didn't need washing.

There is no chance of being invited to that wedding, she told herself sternly. Just put it out of your mind.

But she checked her party shoes to see if they needed polishing.

39

"Fiona," her mother asked the next morning, "why are you moping around the house on a beautiful day like this?"

Fiona went outside to watch for the mail truck and avoid explaining to her mother. She made herself sit on the porch until the carrier had filled the box.

As she brought the mail in, Fiona glanced at it. There was nothing that looked at all like a wedding invitation.

She handed the ads and letters to her mother and watched her toss them on a desk. "Mama, do people ever invite children to weddings?"

"Not if they have good sense," Mrs. Foster said.

Fiona sat on the floor next to the computer desk. "Say a very big wedding."

"I've never been to a big wedding." Mrs. Foster ran her hand over Fiona's hair.

Fiona moved her head, stretching her neck like a cat being stroked. "Have you ever been invited to any wedding?"

"Not really." Mrs. Foster sat back in her chair. "We get wedding announcements a day or two before the ceremony."

Fiona looked up. "What's the difference?"

"The difference is that they don't expect you to come, but they're giving you a chance to send a gift."

"That's terrible!" Fiona was shocked.

Mrs. Foster shrugged. "How about a glass of juice?"

Fiona followed her mother to the kitchen. "Do you ever wish you had had a big wedding?"

Her mother poured two glasses of orange juice and stood by the sink, looking thoughtful. "We more or less eloped. Your father was just out of school, with only a part-time job in a hardware store. My parents were always telling me he'd never amount to anything. And *his* parents were always trying to set him up with the daughters of their friends."

Fiona wondered how many other dark secrets her mother had never told her. *"Why?"*

Mrs. Foster leaned with her elbows on the counter. "I suppose, just like my parents, they wanted their kid to marry somebody rich and gorgeous and unbelievably wonderful. So there was nobody who could sincerely give us a wedding."

Fiona felt stricken. "Mama, that is *sad.*"

"We didn't feel sad. My parents came to like your father, and I get along with his folks." Mrs. Foster took a sip of juice, but she seemed to be thinking of something else.

"Did you at least go out to dinner or anything after you got married?" Fiona prompted.

Mrs. Foster shook her head. "No. I was coming down with a cold."

Fiona could see that talking to her mother was not going to make her feel any better.

It *was* beautiful outside, warm, with a breeze that strayed over Fiona's face. Tomorrow will be a perfect day for an outdoor wedding, she thought. She scuffed along the sidewalk, then stopped. Why can't I just put the whole dumb thing out of my mind? Why do I keep pretending that maybe, somehow, the Lawsons will invite me or my folks? Even people who *know* my parents send them announcements that really mean "don't come"!

Fiona sat down on the grass, not even caring that it was a neighbor's lawn. She wanted to protect her parents from a world so cold it never invited them anywhere.

That's it, of course, she thought, getting up and walking on. It runs in my family. I happened to be born to people who never get invited anywhere, people who have to take a class to learn how to speak up for themselves.

Even if I took a class, it would be hard to come right out and say, "I want to come to your sister's wedding." If I said it to somebody like Barbara, *she'd* probably come right out and say, "No."

The thing to do is figure out how to go after what you want without risking being turned down.

Fiona walked on, thinking so hard she was barely aware of where she was going.

Suppose several guests have called to say they can't come to the wedding. Barbara's parents might be *looking* for people to invite. They might decide it wouldn't do any harm to let her ask a few of her closest friends who could be counted on to behave.

I'm not one of Barbara's closest friends.

But Pauline is.

While I'm out, I should drop over and see how Pauline is feeling, Fiona decided.

She slowed down even more. I know why I'm doing this. I'm doing this because just maybe Barbara has invited her to the wedding. She might still have a touch of flu, but not want to let Barbara down. Pauline's a good person to practice being assertive with. I could say, "Listen, you're not letting anybody down if you don't go to a wedding." Then I could say, "I'd give anything to go." The word would get back to Barbara, and she might ask her parents to invite me, if she couldn't find anybody else.

On her way to Pauline's, Fiona bought a frozen juice bar on a stick. It seemed like a sensible present for somebody who was just getting over stomach flu.

A sensible present, but not on a hot day, she realized, as she climbed the Cahills' porch steps, holding up the bar like an Olympic torch. It's pretty embarrassing to ring somebody's bell with purple juice running down your hand.

She knocked with her left fist.

Mrs. Cahill opened the door. She was a sturdy-looking woman with a square face and short, straight, brown hair. Whenever Fiona saw her, Mrs. Cahill was wearing flat-heeled shoes and a cotton skirt and blouse—Fiona's mother usually wore jeans and a T-shirt when she was working in the yard, or the house, or her office.

43

Mrs. Cahill, Fiona thought, looked like a mother who had enough money to spend her time at dog shows—a person who knew about horses and didn't care anything about fashions.

Seeing Fiona with a melting fruit bar, Mrs. Cahill drew back a little. "Pauline! You'd better come out here!"

While Fiona was wondering whether it would look tackier to lick her wrist or just let the juice run down her arm, Pauline appeared beside her mother.

Pauline did not look sick. Pauline looked a little pale, but she always did. She was an inch shorter than Fiona, and fine boned, with short, dark, curly hair and brown eyes.

"Here." Fiona handed her the bar. "Flu present."

"Oh." Pauline held the stick at arm's length.

"Let me go get a bowl," Mrs. Cahill said.

Left alone with Pauline on the porch, Fiona advised, "You'd better lick it."

"It'll fall off the stick."

"Could I wash my hand?"

Pauline nodded, watching the purple juice fall in slow plops onto the porch.

While Fiona was turning on the front-yard hose, Mrs. Cahill came out holding a bowl. Pauline dropped the bar in it, wrapper and all.

"I'll just put it in the freezer to . . . freshen up." Mrs. Cahill carried the bowl back into the house.

Pauline came down onto the grass and washed her arm under the hose.

"How do you feel?" Fiona asked.

"Okay." Pauline turned off the faucet.

"I mean, normal?"

"Pretty much." Pauline sat on a dry part of the lawn. "Thanks for the fruit bar."

Fiona sat beside her. "They're kind of nice before they refreeze all the way. When they're mushy, you can eat them with a spoon." The thing to do is let Pauline bring up the wedding, so she won't think I care about being invited, Fiona told herself firmly.

"Yeah."

But not knowing was more than Fiona could bear. "So are you going to Barbara's sister's wedding?"

"I'm one of the flower girls."

Fiona could feel her face get hot. "You never told me."

"I was at camp, or home throwing up."

There was no reason to feel so surprised, or so downcast, Fiona told herself. Pauline and Barbara were best friends, after all.

"A flower girl."

"Sure. My mother and Barbara's grew up together. The Lawsons say I'm like one of their own kids."

Fiona stood. "Well, I'd better get going." She just wanted to be in her own room, where she could keep telling herself she shouldn't feel bad, without having

45

to pretend she didn't. "I only came by to bring you a fruit bar."

That was it, of course, Fiona thought, walking home. Pauline and Barbara had grown up together. Their *parents* had grown up together. People who grow up together naturally invite one another to everything.

She wondered how it would feel to live in the town where your parents grew up. You'd know everybody, so you'd know more what to expect from them. Mainly, it would feel cozy, like hanging out with your own dog.

After breakfast the next morning, Fiona took a bath and combed her hair and put the comb in the shiny white plastic purse her grandmother had sent her.

She went downstairs and told her parents, "I'm going over to Barbara's."

"In a party dress and patent-leather shoes, with a purse?" her father asked.

Her mother looked up from the editorial page. "Isn't Barbara's sister getting married today? I read the story in the paper last week."

"That's not for hours yet," Fiona told her.

Mrs. Foster's voice was firm. "Fiona, you are not to get in the way, understand? If those people even look busy, you come right home."

Before Fiona reached the front door, she heard her father ask, "Why is she all dressed up like that?"

"At her age, who knows? The Lawsons will shoo her right home the minute she gets there, anyway."

Fiona shut the front door behind her, wondering

46

why parents figured children couldn't hear anything beyond three feet.

She felt nervous at the idea of being shooed away by the Lawsons. It's something I'll have to get used to, she told herself sternly. People who grow up together probably get shooed home by one another's parents all the time.

Besides, I'm not going to hang around.

It would be a lot of effort for a person just getting over stomach flu to bathe and dress and walk down an aisle. Poor Pauline. At this very moment her parents might be calling the Lawsons to say she was feeling woozy from the excitement, and scared of throwing up in public.

Seeing Fiona all dressed up, the Lawsons would probably ask her right away if she'd consider being a flower girl.

She walked a little faster and then slowed down. While she wanted to arrive in plenty of time, she didn't want to look sweaty.

Barbara was sitting on her front-porch swing, wearing white shoes with straps and a pink dress with an embroidered sash.

"You can't stay," she greeted Fiona. "My sister's getting married."

Fiona stopped on the first porch step. "Oh. Yeah. That's today, isn't it?" She eased up the other steps. "Do you want to play for a while first?"

"I'm not supposed to *move*. I'm a *flower* girl. If I got

my dress messed up, that would ruin the whole wedding." Barbara nodded at Oliver, who stood in his stroller wearing a pale-blue knit suit. "I even have to make sure *he* doesn't get dirty."

Fiona didn't sit down, because that would look like hanging around. Also, she didn't want to wrinkle her skirt. "Let's walk around back."

"Are you kidding? The wedding cake is on the table, and all the punch and stuff. You think I'd let Oliver near that? Already I'm in trouble. My cat got into my sister's room. There's hair all over the wedding gown."

"Is the orchestra here yet?" It can't hurt to keep talking a minute longer, Fiona reasoned. If Pauline's parents had just called, the Lawsons could glance out a front window and say, "Thank goodness! There's Fiona, all neat and clean. Maybe she wouldn't mind being a flower girl."

Barbara evened out her sock ruffles. "They've been here for hours. So has my uncle Frank, with his accordion. I know he's going to sing. He always does. Nobody's ever able to stop him. Listen, you'd better leave, Fiona, before the bridesmaids start coming."

The only hope left, Fiona knew, was that the Lawsons would need a flower girl while she was still in sight.

As she turned to go, she noticed a beetle in a corner of the porch overhang. "Oh, no!" she gasped. "He's walking right into a spiderweb!"

"*Spider?*" Barbara leaped out of her chair. "Yick! *Where?*"

"Hey, come on. Spiders have to eat, just like everybody else." Fiona always felt sorry for spiders, spinning such beautiful, careful webs, only to have them swept away by brooms and hoses and wind.

The spider was lovely to look at, striped brown and gold, big as Fiona's fingernail. While she didn't want to annoy a large spider, she knew she couldn't let him eat this beetle. It wouldn't hurt the spider to miss a meal. It would certainly hurt the beetle to *be* a meal.

Taking her comb from her purse, Fiona climbed onto the porch ledge.

She bent her head back and looked up.

The beetle was already caught in the outside threads of the web, waving his feelers hopelessly as the spider rushed toward him.

Standing on tiptoe, Fiona flicked the beetle free with her comb.

"*Fiona Foster, get off that ledge!*" It was Mrs. Lawson's voice, from inside the house.

Losing her balance, Fiona dropped the comb and swung her arms wildly. She managed to land on her feet, not even wrinkling her dress.

But she had a feeling it didn't matter how she looked, now.

Fiona hunkered down on her heels to peer at the porch floor. "Where's the beetle?" There was no point in saving a bug only to have it get stepped on.

Oliver stretched up in his stroller and peered, too.

"Aaagh!" Barbara cried. "It's in your hair! Fiona, it's in your hair!"

"Barbara!" Mrs. Lawson yelled from inside. "You stop that screaming! And whatever Fiona's doing, send her home!"

As Fiona reached up, feeling for the beetle in her hair, Oliver leaned forward in his stroller.

"*He's* got it!" Barbara's voice was a low and desperate rasp. "Oliver grabbed it off your head!" She squatted in front of the stroller. "*Give it here!*"

Oliver kept his hand closed.

"Oliver," his sister whispered furiously, "do you know what happens to small children who carry bugs to weddings?"

Oliver clapped his fist to his mouth.

As Barbara grabbed his arm, he opened his empty hand.

"*Spit it out!*" she hissed.

"Don't upset him!" Fiona begged. "You want him to swallow?"

Seizing her brother's chin, Barbara pulled down on it. "Open up."

"Wait! If you open his mouth, the beetle might run away from the light." Fiona could see that this was a bad, bad time to be hanging around the Lawsons' porch. "I'll just go on home, and you get your mother."

"My mother? My *mother*?" Barbara's voice got high, but not loud. "My mother has a sick headache. My sister has cried all morning. My father says that if I grow up and want a wedding, he'll never speak to me. You want me to go in there and tell them I let Oliver eat a beetle covered in spiderweb?"

"I don't think he ate it," Fiona murmured hopefully. "I think it's still in his mouth."

"You *think*. *You* think! How do you think I feel with a beetle in my brother's mouth?"

"How do you think the beetle feels?" Fiona demanded.

A taxi pulled up at the curb, and a tall woman with lavender-tinted white hair got out. She wore a tiny blue hat with a veil, a pale-blue dress, and white gloves.

Barbara made a little whimpering noise in her throat. "Grandmother Lawson!"

Fiona knew it was too late to escape. Besides, she couldn't leave the beetle trapped in Oliver's mouth.

"I'll get her into the house," Barbara whispered. "You try to get the beetle."

Easing closer to Barbara, Fiona watched Grandmother Lawson come up the porch steps.

She'll know. If I look half as guilty as Barbara does, her grandmother will know something's going on.

"There's my big girl!" Grandmother Lawson bent to hug Barbara. "Don't look so *tense*, sweetheart. All you have to do is carry a basket and not trip."

51

Letting Barbara go, she lifted Oliver out of his stroller. "Here's my baby lamb. Give Grandma a big kiss." She pursed her lips not an inch from his.

"You don't want him to do that, Grandma!" Barbara's voice was strained but sincere.

Barbara's parents came out the front door. Putting one arm around Grandmother Lawson and another around Oliver, Mr. Lawson hugged them.

"You look terrible," Barbara's grandmother greeted Mrs. Lawson.

"I feel terrible," Barbara's mother said. "I have a sick headache and a daughter upstairs saying she wants to change her mind." She peered at Oliver. "What has he got in his mouth, Barbara?"

"Teeth," Barbara said. "Grandma, why don't you just put him down."

"Not until I get my kiss." Grandmother Lawson made little chirpy kissing sounds right by Oliver's face.

Arnold, Barbara's cat, came bounding up the porch steps to rub against Mr. Lawson's dark-blue trousers.

Barbara's father threw his arms out at his sides. "He hates me. That's all. The cat hates me."

"Nonsense. It's only cat hair, Walter. Where's your clothes brush?" Grandmother Lawson plopped Oliver into his stroller.

Spitting out the beetle, Oliver held it up to her. Being wet, it slipped out of his hand.

Arnold pounced. As Arnold batted the beetle to the

floor, Barbara grabbed him and Fiona snatched up the still and soggy beetle.

Mr. Lawson seized Barbara by the shoulders, and his voice made Fiona edge toward the porch steps. *"How did a beetle get into your brother's mouth?"*

Fiona reminded herself that it was more or less her fault. She reminded herself that Barbara had told her to go home. "Um . . . it was in my hair."

"Fiona Foster, what in the world were you doing with a beetle in your hair?" Mrs. Lawson demanded.

"You get off this porch, young lady," Mr. Lawson ordered Fiona. "And don't you ever come around here again with beetles in your hair."

Fiona hurried down the stairs and along the walk, not looking back, wondering what the three grown-ups were saying about her.

She thought of all the hours she'd spent wishing, of polishing her shoes and getting dressed up. She'd even been willing to risk getting shooed home, but she'd never expected to be disgraced, to be *ordered* away.

What hurt most was remembering how hard she'd hoped to be invited to this wedding.

Maybe being invited wasn't the main thing, she thought. Maybe not being left out was what really mattered.

She headed for the park, feeling the beetle still and damp in her closed hand. She didn't dare open her fist to see how he was. With her luck, and his, he'd manage to crash to the sidewalk on his head.

At the park, she sat under a tree and opened her hand on the grass, palm up. For a while the beetle lay in her hand, waving his feelers feebly.

Fiona nudged him onto his belly with the forefinger of her other hand.

He staggered to the side of her thumb and fell off, then pottered away in the grass.

"Fiona Foster!" her mother greeted her when she walked in the back door. "What do you mean strolling in here late for lunch with grass stains all over your dress? And what is that sticky mess in your hair?"

Fiona touched her head. "Spiderweb."

"I'm not even sure I want to know how it got there," Mr. Foster said.

"I saved a beetle."

"Where is it?" her father asked.

"In the park."

"Oh, good." He went on clearing the table.

"Go take your dress off," Mrs. Foster told Fiona. "Soak it in cold water. Then you'll have to wash it by hand."

Upstairs, Fiona swished her dress through the water in the bathroom sink. Saving bugs is important work, she thought. You just can't expect any thanks.

While her dress soaked, she went down to the kitchen and made herself a cold bean sandwich.

If either of her parents came in and said, "Oh, Fiona! Is that all you're having?" she would say very quietly, "I just feel like a cold bean sandwich."

A person can take just so long eating a cold bean sandwich. When Fiona finished, she tidied up after herself, even brushing every single crumb off the table.

Since nobody in her family showed any interest in what she ate, or whether, she went outside and filled her dog dish. Then she sat beside it on the porch.

If anybody should care enough about his or her only child to look out the window and say, "Oh, sweetie. What are you doing just sitting all alone by the dog dish?" she would simply shrug and say softly, "Nothing."

By now the wedding was nearly over, if the bride hadn't changed her mind. Barbara and Pauline had had their pictures taken in their flower-girl outfits. Hundreds of people in pale fluttery dresses and light-colored suits were finishing off the punch and sandwiches and cake. Maybe the orchestra was still playing. Or maybe they had quit, and the uncle was singing, and everybody was saying in surprise, "But he's *marvelous!*"

Fiona found a few leaves on the porch and floated them in the water, in case a bee fell in again when she wasn't watching. But suppose that a dog dropped by and was so thirsty he'd drink the water, leaves and all, and get one stuck in his throat? She fished the leaves out one by one, and emptied the dish, and refilled it. Then she took it back to the porch again and sat beside it.

She tried to remember all the verses of "America the Beautiful" and "They're Changing Guard at Buckingham Palace."

Barbara came across the street, pushing Oliver's stroller.

Oliver was not in it.

Fiona had never heard of a poisonous beetle. Oliver hadn't swallowed his anyway. *But it had been in his mouth a long time.*

Fiona's eyes felt hot and her hands felt cold as she watched Barbara haul the stroller up the porch steps. "Where's Oliver?"

"Down for his nap." From one of the sacks in the stroller Barbara took little white boxes and paper napkins with silver bells printed on them. She set the boxes on the floor, one by one, and opened them.

The first was filled with mixed nuts, the second with ribbon sandwiches, the third with pink and green and yellow mints. In the last box were two wedges of wedding cake. The frosting was hardly mashed, so Fiona could make out parts of the pale-pink icing flowers.

"It was a pretty good wedding." Barbara seemed ill at ease. "Once you were out of the way, everybody forgot about the beetle. Or at least they were too busy to think about it."

She's apologizing! Fiona thought, astonished. In her

own grumpy way she's trying to let me know she's sorry I got blamed for everything.

Barbara picked the cashews out of the mixed nuts. "So how's the beetle?" she asked casually.

"Fine. I left him in the park." Fiona sniffed a ribbon sandwich carefully. Satisfied none of the filling layers were pastel-tinted fish, she took a bite.

"How come you run into more bugs than most people?" Barbara asked.

Fiona swallowed the bite. "I don't. I just notice them more."

From upstairs, Mrs. Foster called, "Fiona, get your dress washed so I can use the bathroom basin."

"I have to go anyway. I don't want to miss how they finally shut up Uncle Frank." Reaching into the second sack of the stroller, Barbara took out a wreath of pink and white flowers. "It's what I wore on my head." She plopped it down on the porch railing.

Fiona felt her face get warm. She didn't know where to look, or what to say. In her whole life, nobody had ever given her flowers.

"I'm glad you saved the beetle," Barbara muttered, and stomped away before Fiona could do something really embarrassing, like thanking her.

Fiona finished the last of the nuts, nested the empty boxes, stuffed the napkins in them, and took them around to the trash can. She left the cake and sandwich crumbs for any birds that might drop by.

*　　*　　*

As Fiona came up the hall stairs, her mother looked over the banister. "Where in the world did you get a wreath?"

"Here." Handing the flowers to Mrs. Foster, Fiona walked past her into the bathroom.

While she was kneading water out of her dress, she saw her mother behind her, in the mirror.

"Thank you for the flowers."

"You're welcome."

"That doesn't mean you can let your dress drip on the floor."

Fiona rolled the dress in a towel.

"I suppose there's a story behind all this." Her mother sat on the edge of the tub.

"Everything that happened?" Fiona asked.

Mrs. Foster nodded. "It's part of the mother business. I only hope I'm up to it."

Fiona reached for a second towel. "Well, it didn't turn out too bad, so why don't I start with the ending. That will make it easier for you to hear the rest. . . ."

4

"The end of summer is a scary time," Fiona told her mother at lunch.

"Scary?" Mrs. Foster sprinkled a few oyster crackers into her soup. "I always thought of it more as sad."

"I'm thinking about school starting."

Mrs. Foster smiled. "Maybe a little scary. But I remember it as exciting, too. Everything was *new*—my shoes and my clothes and even my pencils." She looked as if she were gazing somewhere beyond the backyard. "I'd pick up my friends early and we'd get to the school yard and hang out in front of the building and look everybody over. You know, I still remember the smell of grade-school corridors—chalk dust and metal lockers."

"Does metal have a smell?"

"School lockers do."

"But you'd lived in that town for years." Fiona stirred her soup more and more slowly. "You knew the school, and the kids. What I'm talking about is wondering who'll walk to school with you, and whether they'll stick with you once you get there. What if you get put in classes with nobody you know? What if you can't find your homeroom? What if you can't find the *bathroom*?"

"What is also scary," her mother said, very softly, "is sending your kid out into the world, and not being able to go with her and protect her. But I know it makes sense. Otherwise we'd have a lot of parents walking their twenty-year-old kids to their first day of work."

Fiona pictured herself, a grown-up woman, with her mother leading her by the hand into a big office building.

"Now look what you did." She blotted her place mat with her paper napkin.

"If you never remember anything else I've taught you," her mother said, trying to keep a solemn face, "remember never to laugh with a full soupspoon in your hand."

Not even your mother can keep worries out of your head, Fiona realized at bedtime. They keep squeezing in. If Howard and Larry and Barbara and Pauline walk to school with me, fine. But suppose Barbara and Pauline leave for school early, without waiting for anybody? I can't walk to school with two *boys*!

Then an even more dreadful thought struck her.

What if Pauline's flu comes back, and Howard and Larry and Barbara catch it? That would mean I'd have to walk to school alone! And what if my clothes are so wrong nobody will want to sit next to me in class?

Fiona did not sleep well that night.

Fiona had avoided the Lawsons' house ever since Barbara's sister's wedding, so in the morning she went over to the Cahills'. Barbara and Pauline sat on the porch playing checkers. Oliver stood in his stroller painting his face with a graham cracker. He was the only one who looked up at Fiona.

She decided the thing to do was be assertive and get right down to business. "So. What are you guys going to wear to school the first day?"

"Once you start to move a checker, you can't take it back," Barbara told Pauline.

"I didn't move it," Pauline said. "I just touched it, and then I changed my mind."

Fiona knew you don't get anywhere interrupting people who are having an argument. She waited.

"You did move it." Barbara squinted her eyes ominously at Pauline.

"It doesn't count if I didn't take my fingers off it," Pauline declared.

"I saw you," Barbara insisted. "You started to pick it up, and then you put it down again."

Pauline snatched up the board, scattering checkers

61

over her porch. "There. Now I moved them all!"

Leaping to her feet, Barbara snatched Oliver out of his stroller and led him down the stairs, pulling the stroller *bump bump bump* down after them.

"And stay away!" Pauline yelled.

While it was a pretty interesting quarrel, Fiona didn't really have time to appreciate it. She had more important things to deal with. "So have you decided what you're going to wear the first day of school?" she asked Pauline as Barbara disappeared down the street.

"Are you going to help me collect these checkers or are you just going to stand there?"

Fiona could feel herself getting more angry with each checker she picked up, but she told herself there was no sense losing her temper. She was here on business. "So what are you going to wear?"

Pauline looked at her for the second time. "What?"

"The first day of school. What will you wear?"

"Who cares?" Pauline reached for the checkers Fiona had gathered.

Leaning over the porch rail, Fiona dropped them in the hedge. "Pick up your own dumb checkers." She made herself walk down the stairs slowly and deliberately, without even looking back.

That took a lot of nerve, she thought, rather pleased with herself as she headed home.

But it's going to take a lot more to talk to Pauline again anytime soon.

*   *   *

"I wonder what people in this town wear on the first day of school," Fiona mused at dinner that evening.

"What they wear in any other town, I'm sure," her mother said. "Pass the potatoes."

"Maybe not," Fiona said. "And you don't know until you've been through the first day at any school at least once."

Mr. Foster lifted a bowl and gazed warily at the potatoes. "Why are there lumps in them?"

"You're the one who cooked them," Mrs. Foster said. "We can look in the paper," she told Fiona, "and see what the stores are advertising."

"What they're advertising might not be what kids are buying," Fiona pointed out. "I'd sure feel stupid if I showed up looking different from everybody else."

Mr. Foster poked the potatoes with a serving spoon. "I took them right out of the freezer. They didn't have lumps then."

"I wish we'd never moved here!" Fiona said.

He looked at her in surprise. "What in the world brought that on!"

"You're not *listening* to me. Nobody listens to me," Fiona said.

"I was listening, sweetie," her mother told her.

"Yeah, but I need you both to listen."

"You're right." Her father looked very serious. "You do. What were you saying?"

"I don't feel like saying it all over again." The problem, Fiona thought, is getting anybody to listen *in time*. But he was a good father, and he tried.

The next morning after breakfast, Fiona wandered into her mother's office. "Are you going to take a break soon?"

"Mmm." Mrs. Foster kept her eyes on the computer monitor. "Aren't you going to go out and play?"

"Am I just going to wear whatever clothes I have?"

Mrs. Foster looked at her. "To play in?"

"On the first day of school."

"Honey, I've got to finish this project this week. As soon as it's done, I'll give all my attention to buying your school clothes. We'll have a big shopping day—how's that?"

"School starts in five days," Fiona murmured, in case her mother wasn't keeping track.

"That's plenty of time."

"Not when you don't even know what everybody else will be wearing."

Her mother pushed back her chair and turned. "Fiona, this is not like dressing for a royal wedding. A simple dress always looks right at school, or a skirt and sweater."

"If it's a hot day, a sweater would itch me."

"All right. A skirt and blouse, with a sweater over them."

"If it's a cold day, I'd need a coat instead."

Mrs. Foster pressed two fingers of each hand against her temples. "Fiona, what is it? Are you jealous of my work? Or can't you resist the urge to torment me when I'm under pressure?"

Fiona trudged outside and sat beside her dog dish. What a thing to say to your own child, she thought. She sat at the top of the porch steps. Being an only child, in a new town, and nobody's best friend, is about as lonely as anybody can get, she decided. Unless you have parents who are working under pressure. She gazed at the empty dog dish. Unless you have not so much as a turtle you can talk to.

She was running her finger around the bottom of the dog dish when her mother came out, wearing a skirt and shirt and even stockings. "All right. I'll work late tonight. Go change your clothes and we'll buy your school things."

"We can't do that," Fiona said.

"Fiona, you've been nagging me all morning about your school wardrobe!"

"We can't *buy* anything until we know what everybody else is going to wear."

"We'll ask the clerks." Mrs. Foster spoke slowly and carefully.

"They'll try to sell us what they wore when they were kids," Fiona protested, feeling more and more upset.

"Believe me, we did not wear bearskins when I was a girl. Once you decide what it is you want to do, we

65

can talk about shopping, but not before." Turning, Mrs. Foster stalked back into the house.

Boy, Fiona thought, she *is* tense.

She sat on the porch awhile, feeling miserable. There was the first cool hint of fall in the air, and fall meant school, and school was something that had to be faced.

I've got three choices, Fiona thought. I can go ask Barbara what she's going to wear, and her parents may remember the beetle in Oliver's mouth the minute they see me. I can go shopping with no idea what people here wear on the first day of school. Or I can go back to Pauline's.

Fiona went into her mother's office. Mrs. Foster had changed back into jeans and a T-shirt and sneakers.

"I guess I'll go over to Pauline's," Fiona said.

"Be back for lunch."

She already sounds calm and reasonable, Fiona thought, relieved. By lunchtime, she'll be her old self.

Mrs. Cahill looked harried as she opened her front door. "Pauline is in her room," she said, and walked away.

Pauline was sitting on her bed taking price tags off new underwear. She watched warily as Fiona stood by the desk.

"So," Fiona ventured, trying to sound casual but not daring to sit down, "what are you wearing the first day of school?"

"A dress, or a skirt and blouse, if it's warm. If it's

cool, I'll wear a skirt and sweater. My mother says you always dress up for the first day."

Fiona watched Pauline put the tags in one pile and the pins in another. "Did you get anything new besides underwear?"

"Sure. A dress, and some skirts and pants and tops, and a coat."

Fiona thought how lucky Pauline was to have a mother who took her shopping early. "That's neat."

"It's a pain."

Fiona was surprised. "What do you mean? You got all those great clothes."

"That was in the morning. Two days ago. Then we had lunch downtown."

"In a *restaurant*?"

Pauline nodded. "We went with Barbara and her mother."

Of course, Fiona thought. After all, Barbara's and Pauline's mothers had grown up together. Fiona could picture them, buying clothes they all knew looked right. She imagined them, surrounded by packages, sitting in a restaurant. It would be a nice restaurant, with a padded seat around three sides of the table, and huge menus. "Did you get dessert, too?"

"Sundaes."

"The kind with little paper parasols stuck in them?"

"Just maraschino cherries and walnuts on the whipped cream."

67

"Then what?" Though it stung to hear about the shopping trip, Fiona couldn't help asking.

"Then we shopped for school shoes." Pauline's voice was flat.

Fiona realized she had no idea what kind of shoes everybody wore to school in this town. "What did you get?"

"Anything I like, my mother says will ruin my feet. Then she has the clerk bring the same horrible old gunboat shoes as every year. She makes me try them on, then she accuses me of sulking because I won't say how I like them. Can you imagine if I said how I hated them in front of the clerk? We go to another store and another, and go through the same thing. By the time we left the fifth shoe department, my mother hauled me around behind the escalators, and she almost got *violent*."

"*Why?*"

"I hadn't even said anything. I think that's what set her off. It happened last year, too."

"What about Barbara?"

"Same thing. Same shoes. She got so depressed, she stopped talking too. Then, in the parking lot, all Barbara said was that she'd probably have to go to school in bedroom slippers, and her mother really lost it. It was embarrassing, the way she yelled."

Fiona was impressed, but she kept her mind on what was important. "So what shoes did you get?"

"None."

"Neither of you?"

"It was just the same last year. They keep making us try on those old gunboat shoes. They tell us that when we're grown, we'll be grateful that they made us wear them. They go on about refusing to let us ruin our feet. They tell us any of the shoes we like will give us bunions. Bunions. Last year, my mother even dragged me into the women's lounge and took off her shoes and made me look at her bunions! She said she got them because her mother didn't force her to wear sensible shoes."

This sounded truly gruesome, but Fiona had to know. "What are bunions?"

"Hard lumps on the outside of your big-toe joints. Really gross. But not so bad as wearing those shoes they try to force on you."

I don't even know about shopping for *shoes*, Fiona realized. "What will you wear to school, then?"

"You think mothers give up? They dragged us shoe shopping again yesterday. It was horrible, and they got even more furious, and we're stuck with the shoes they want, just like last year."

Fiona felt even more anxious. "Could I see them?"

"Why?"

"So I'll know what I don't want."

Pauline nodded toward the shoe box on her desk. "I won't even let them in my closet."

Fiona opened the box. She made herself take out one of the shoes. They were just like the ones her

69

mother had bought her the year before. "Did you feel awful wearing them to school last year?"

"A lot of other kids have fussy mothers."

When Fiona got home, her mother was making a salad.

Fiona watched her rinse the lettuce. "Do I have to wear that same dumb kind of lace-up leather shoes to school this year?"

"Oxfords. Hand me a tomato."

"The kind that look really gross."

"No, a nice round firm red one."

Fiona handed her mother a round firm red tomato. "I mean shoes."

Mrs. Foster put down her paring knife. "Fiona, what has gotten into you? You're suddenly clothes crazy."

"Why do they have to be lace-up leather?"

"Your feet need support." Mrs. Foster ran cold water over the tomato and put it on the chopping board.

"They don't have support all summer. And why leather? Why skin a cow to make shoes that kids hate?"

Mrs. Foster cut the tomato into wedges. "Leather lets your feet breathe."

"*Breathe*? Feet *breathe*?"

Her mother set down the knife again. "You may want junk shoes now, but someday you'll thank me for making you wear decent shoes. If I let you wear junk, you'd turn around when you're forty and blame me because you have bunions."

Fiona realized she had never really looked at her mother's feet. "Do you have bunions?"

"Didn't you ever notice?"

"Will you turn around and blame your mother when you're forty?"

Mrs. Foster cut the little roots off the green onions, and then cut off the grassy tops. "My mother, poor woman, forced me to wear sensible shoes until I was twelve. I will never forgive myself for what I put her through, year after year. Every year we went home with her not speaking to me."

Fiona leaned on the counter. "So how did you end up with bunions?"

"Your mother doesn't take you shoe shopping after you're twelve! You'd be ruined if anybody you knew saw you shopping with your *mother*."

"Did you ever thank her?" Fiona asked.

"For what?" Mrs. Foster chopped the onion into tiny pieces.

"For making you wear sensible shoes until you were twelve."

Tossing the onions into a bowl, Mrs. Foster turned to face Fiona. "How would you feel about shopping for school clothes with your father?"

Fiona suspected that her father would not know a girl's sensible shoe from a junk shoe even if her mother drew him a diagram. She nodded slowly.

But her mother looked at her, narrow eyed. "No. No, I think I had better take you. Once it's over, I'll thank myself." She tossed the lettuce and tomato into the bowl. "I'll take tomorrow afternoon off."

"We could go early in the day, and maybe have lunch downtown."

"Oh, honey, I'm going to have to work straight through the morning."

Fiona sighed.

The next afternoon was warm, and Mrs. Foster kept the car windows down. How much money do you need to have before you get a car with air conditioning? Fiona wondered.

The mall's parking lots were so crowded, they drove around and around before Mrs. Foster found a space. As they walked across the acres of concrete, Fiona could feel the heat shimmering off the pavement.

Molberry's was crowded and noisy. In the girlswear department, Fiona and her mother looked through rack after rack of skirts. Then they stood in line for a dressing room.

By the time Fiona had tried on three skirts, she felt hot and tired and grumpy. One skirt made her stomach look fat. One felt scratchy. When she put on the third, she said, "I look like somebody in a fun-house mirror."

"All right." Her mother gathered up the skirts Fiona had tried. She took them out to a clerk while Fiona dressed.

Fiona came out and handed her mother the third

skirt. Her mother put in on a counter and headed out of the girlswear department.

Fiona trotted after her. "What about sweaters? What about blouses?"

Her mother kept walking.

"Maybe we could get a soda and relax," Fiona suggested.

"We're going to get shoes, and then I'll see whether I'm up to any more shopping with you."

It was a bad sign when your mother was annoyed before you even *started* to look at shoes.

Grown-ups and children milled around in the children's shoe department. All the chairs were taken, and all the stools had people sitting on them.

With her mother, Fiona edged through the crowds to the TAKE A NUMBER sign. Mrs. Foster pulled off a number card. Then they wormed their way close enough to a table to see the shoes on it.

Fiona put her hand on a flat-heeled navy-blue shoe with a narrow T-strap. "This one's not bad."

"It wouldn't last two weeks," her mother said.

They made their way through the crush to the racks on the walls.

"How about that one?" Fiona asked.

"It looks like something a rock star would wear."

"Really?" Fiona reached for the shoe, but her mother took her firmly by the hand and led her to the next rack. "Here we are."

"Mother!" The shoe was identical to Pauline's. "It's horrible!"

"It's just what you wore last year."

"I know! It's horrible!"

"I am thinking of your feet. Ten years from now, do you want them looking like gnarled branches?"

"I'm going to have feet like tree branches if I don't wear that one particular awful shoe?"

"Don't get smart," Mrs. Foster warned. "We'll just try them on. You'll see that they look perfectly fine once you wear them." Suddenly, she grabbed Fiona's wrist and yanked her almost off her feet.

A woman and a girl were just getting out of their seats. "You'll thank me when you're older," the woman told the girl as they followed a clerk carrying a shoe box.

Mrs. Foster shoved Fiona into the nearest seat and plopped into the adjoining one, a second ahead of a woman with two boys.

Clerks rushed in and out of the stockroom carrying stacks of boxes. Now and then one would finish with a customer and call out a number, and some man or woman would yell, "Here!"

Fiona looked at the number on her mother's card. "Why don't we come back some other time?"

"After waiting this long?" Mrs. Foster looked weary, and her hair frizzed around her face. "Besides, it'll be worse later in the week."

Fiona thought about Pauline and Barbara. At least

74

they'd had lunch in a restaurant, and sundaes with whipped cream and nuts, before they had gone through this.

At last a clerk called out, "Seventy-three!" and Fiona's mother cried, "Here! Here!" To Fiona she said, "Take off your shoes."

The clerk was a thin, tired-looking man of about forty who walked as if his feet hurt. He didn't greet Fiona or her mother, but looked around, in vain, for an empty stool.

"We want to see something in a nice, sensible school shoe," Mrs. Foster told him.

"Size?" he asked.

"Don't you *measure*?" There was an edge to Mrs. Foster's voice.

He took a ruler with a sliding section from his hip pocket, and Fiona stood while he measured her foot.

"Saddle oxfords?" he asked Mrs. Foster.

She nodded. "White."

Fiona waited until the clerk walked away before she spoke to her mother. "You didn't even ask me!"

"They're just what you had last year," Mrs. Foster said calmly. "They'll go with anything."

Fiona watched other people in the department, looking for some girl her age getting decent shoes that she could point out to her mother. But all around her parents and children were either arguing in low tones or looking miserable.

The clerk returned with two shoe boxes. Grabbing

a stool a woman had just vacated, he pulled it in front of Fiona. She sat silently while he put a white saddle oxford on her and tied the laces.

"Stand up," her mother told her.

Fiona stood.

"How does it feel?" her mother asked her.

Fiona thought of Pauline dragged behind the escalators. "I don't know."

Mrs. Foster knelt and poked her thumb down on the toe of the shoe. "Do you have it in a half size longer?" she asked the clerk.

He nodded toward the shoe boxes and walked away. Instantly, a man grabbed the empty stool.

"Take off the shoe." Mrs. Foster opened the second box. "Let's try these."

"They're the same as the one I just took off," Fiona protested.

"No. They are"—Mrs. Foster picked up the box—"half a size longer. Give me your left foot."

Fiona extended her left foot toward her mother.

"Keep your skirt down," her mother told her sharply, and put the longer shoe on her. "Stand up."

Fiona stood.

Her mother pressed on the toe of the shoe and felt the sides. "Take a few steps."

Fiona took three steps forward.

"Good." Mrs. Foster kept her eyes on the shoe. "It doesn't slip or slide, and there's room across the toes."

"I would die being seen in it," Fiona declared, but her mother wasn't listening.

"Let me find the clerk while you put on the mate."

Left alone to defend their chairs, Fiona sat quickly in hers. Then she put the boxes on her mother's, feeling like a member of a space expedition left to guard the shuttlecraft against hostile aliens.

What if everybody thinks I'm hogging two chairs? she worried. To avoid meeting anybody's gaze, she reached into the closer box for the mate of the shoe she wore. With any luck, she thought, it will slip or slide or be tight across my toes.

She lifted the shoe from its paper nest.

In the box, something moved.

5

Startled, Fiona jerked back, dropping the shoe.

The movement in the box was very small, and very feeble.

Fiona looked closer.

In the paper nest, huddled against a corner of the box, was a mouse, hardly bigger than her thumb. He was lovely, with his soft, gray, velvety fur and dark, innocent eyes. And he was trembling, too terrified to escape.

Suddenly, Fiona thought of a poem her first-grade teacher back in Kelsey had read the class, a poem by Christina Rossetti, who had been dead over a hundred years. The last stanza flashed into Fiona's head now:

78

The city mouse eats bread and cheese;—
The garden mouse eats what he can;
We will not grudge him seeds and stocks,
Poor little timid furry man.

Fiona had never before remembered that many lines of a poem.

Of course, she'd never before come face to face with a mouse in the shoe department at Molberry's.

She clapped the lid back on the box. Coming toward her was her mother, with the clerk.

Fiona could imagine how it must feel to be as small and scared and hopeless as a mouse in a crowded, roaring store.

Poor little timid furry man.

She got the right saddle oxford on and tied by the time her mother reached her.

"Take a few steps," Mrs. Foster said.

Fiona walked, staying close to their chairs, her eyes on the shoe box.

If she turned down these dreadful shoes, she knew, the clerk would slap them in the box, right on top of the mouse. Certainly, if he saw the mouse, he'd try to kill it. And if it ever got out in the shoe department, there would be a terrible panic. If the hordes didn't trample it, if the clerks didn't corner it, it would surely die of fear.

"How do they feel?" her mother prompted.

79

In the box or out of it, left in this store, the mouse would surely die.

Fiona looked down at her feet. She could not recall ever hating shoes before. But the mouse had only one chance.

"They're okay." She shrugged.

"These will do," Mrs. Foster told the clerk, who was gazing around him while people waved frantically for his attention.

"I'll wear them," Fiona said.

Scooping up Fiona's old shoes, the clerk reached for the box.

"No!" Fiona snatched it up. "I'll carry it, thank you."

The clerk led them to a cash register. While Mrs. Foster signed the charge slip, he dumped Fiona's old shoes into a bag and held it open for her to put the box in.

Shaking her head, Fiona hugged the box closer.

As she headed for the escalators with Fiona, Mrs. Foster said, "This has been a long afternoon. You know, your father's going to be finished work in a few minutes? We'll all go downstairs to the coffee shop for dinner. Then you and I can finish shopping."

"Could we just go home? Right now?"

Mrs. Foster stopped. "Fiona, just a few minutes ago you were after me for a soda. Now I'm going to take you out to dinner."

"I would rather go home."

Mrs. Foster's voice was strained. "There is no point

in driving home and then turning right back around to come pick up your father. He won't want to walk home in this heat."

Fiona shifted the box under her arm. "How about . . . how about we all just go home and grab something to eat, and then we could come back?"

"No." Mrs. Foster's voice was firm. "Once we leave this madhouse, I am not returning."

As shoppers edged around her, Fiona heard a rustling inside the box. She put her free hand on the lid. "I could come back with Dad."

Her mother didn't even seem to notice that they were blocking the aisle. "Fiona, all week you have tormented me to take you shopping. I have taken the afternoon off. I have put up with your sulking through three skirts. I have gone through the horrors of a children's shoe department. Ordinarily, I would never entrust your clothes shopping to a man who wears brown wing-tip shoes and clip-on bow ties. But yes. Yes, your father will finish shopping with you." She took Fiona by the elbow.

Fiona doubled over the shoe box like a football player protecting the ball.

"Whatever this nonsense is, you stop it right now!" Mrs. Foster propelled her onto the escalator.

Mr. Foster was putting spectacle frames on a display carousel as Mrs. Foster marched Fiona into the optical department. "Well"—he smiled—"how was the shopping trip?"

81

."Let's have dinner downstairs," Mrs. Foster greeted him.

"Herb!" he called.

A thin young man in aviator glasses and a brown suit came out from behind a curtain at the rear of the department.

"I'm going to take off," Mr. Foster told him. "You can hold the fort here. If you have time, check over those inventory sheets."

Anxious as she was, Fiona could not help admiring how her father could be so businesslike and agreeable.

As they threaded through the aisles, he put a hand on her shoulder. "So what all did you buy, honey?"

"Shoes," Fiona murmured.

"And what else?"

"Nothing," Mrs. Foster said flatly.

"Shopping all afternoon, and you only got a pair of shoes?" He seemed surprised.

Fiona's mother stopped for a second and closed her eyes.

"Why don't we go on home so I don't scuff them up?" Fiona suggested.

Her father only nudged her onto the DOWN escalator.

At the coffee shop, a waitress showed them right to a booth.

Fiona sat between her parents, shoe box in her lap, both hands planted on the lid.

"Why don't you put that on the floor?" her father asked.

"It's fine." There had been no sound, no movement, in the box since they'd left the optical department, Fiona realized. Could the mouse be resting? Sleeping?

Could he have fainted from lack of oxygen?

"I need to go to the bathroom," Fiona said urgently.

Mr. Foster eased out of the booth and stood, looking resigned.

Mrs. Foster got out the other side. "I'll come with you," she told Fiona. "The way you've been acting, you're going to fool around in there forever if I don't."

The only thing to do was get into a stall and open the lid and hope a few moments of air would revive the mouse . . . without refreshing him so much he'd jump out of the box.

What if he manages to fall into the toilet, and I have to try to fish him out with my mother right there outside the door? I can't sit on the floor. She would surely see I was sitting on the floor.

Fiona stayed where she was. "That's okay."

"She has been like this all afternoon." Mrs. Foster slid back into the booth. "This is what I've had with her all day."

Mr. Foster seated himself again. "Let's just order and try to have a pleasant meal."

"I'm not very hungry," Fiona said.

"Then you can share my dinner," Mr. Foster told her calmly.

I could say I was sick to my stomach, Fiona thought. That would get us out of here. No. No. Mama would *rush* me to the rest room and hold my forehead and make me put down the shoe box and sit with my face over the toilet. *What if the mouse suddenly shoved the lid right off the box?*

Fiona sat, holding the box in her lap, while her parents ordered. She sat while they talked to each other.

Then, knowing what a risk she took, she dipped one hand into her water glass.

"Fiona!" Mrs. Foster admonished her.

Dropping her hand to her lap, Fiona rubbed a wet finger on the box lid, trying to work a little hole in it, just enough for the mouse to get air without getting his head out.

When the waitress brought the soup and salad, Mr. Foster slid his cup of tomato bisque over to Fiona.

"No, thank you."

He peered at her. "Are you sure you feel all right?"

Fiona nodded. If her parents got into a discussion of whether she was sick or just impossible, they'd only be stuck in this coffee shop longer.

Her father took back the soup and her mother began eating the salad.

From the box in Fiona's lap came a new sound.

It was not loud, but it was alarming.

It was the sound of gnawing.

The mouse had decided to chew his way free.

Fiona sat quite still, her hands on the lid. *How long? How long will it take a mouse to eat through a shoe box? What if it happens right here in the booth?*

She imagined the mouse suddenly leaping off her lap, scurrying across the floor, or even the tables, of the crowded coffee shop.

Glancing at her parents, she tried to think of some way to hurry them through dinner.

What if the mouse gets out on the way home? Fiona imagined her mother struggling to keep control of the wheel, with a terrified mouse leaping around in the car.

There was only one thing to do.

"I think we'd better get out of here." She tried to speak low enough so people at the other booths wouldn't hear.

"Fiona . . ." Mrs. Foster glanced at her, exasperated.

"What we have is an emergency." Fiona's face felt damp and her voice wobbled.

Now her mother looked worried. "Do you feel sick?"

"No. I've got a mouse in my lap."

One thing about parents: When you get their attention, you get *all* their attention.

Mrs. Foster dropped her forkful of salad, and Mr. Foster half stood, bumping the table so the water sloshed out of the glasses.

Almost at once Fiona's mother fixed her with a cold, hard glare. "Fiona, that was not funny."

"Mama," Fiona said desperately, "there is a mouse

in this shoe box, eating his way out of it."

Mr. Foster grabbed some bills out of his wallet and threw them on the table. Seizing Fiona, so that she had to shift the box under her other arm, he yanked her out of the booth and rushed from the coffee shop.

When they reached their station wagon, Mrs. Foster unlocked the door. Without a word, she slid behind the wheel and then reached back to unlock the rear door.

Opening it, Mr. Foster shoved Fiona in, then went around to the front passenger side and got in.

As her mother started the engine, Fiona asked uneasily, "You're not going to panic or anything if he gets out, are you?"

Nobody answered.

"You didn't *know* she brought a mouse to the store?" Mr. Foster asked as Mrs. Foster backed out of the parking space.

"I did not think to ask her." Mrs. Foster's voice was low and strained. "You do not think to ask your daughter, before you take her shopping, if she happens to be packing a rodent."

If you bring a mouse to dinner, Fiona told herself, you've got to expect your parents to be upset. What she could not bear was knowing that she had not done the mouse any favor. I rescue him from the shoe department, she thought, and now he's trapped in a box in a car with people who wipe out ants by the hundreds without even thinking about it.

Mouse, she thought, I did not let myself get stuck with the most horrible shoes in the world only to have you get killed. I did not sit through part of the most terrible meal in my life just for you to die.

"He was in the shoe box at the store," she said. "I opened the box to get out the mate of the shoe I had on, and there he was."

"So you kept him." Mrs. Foster's voice was flat.

Fiona felt more sure than she'd felt about anything for as long as she could remember. "What else could I do?" Even to herself her voice sounded almost grown-up. "I'm hundreds of times his size, and hundreds of times smarter. Would you really want a child who would shut the box and leave him? Or would you want him to get out there in Molberry's and cause a stampede?"

"Put something over the box in case he gets out now," Mrs. Foster told Mr. Foster.

"Like what?" he asked.

"Your jacket, anything."

"Then we'd have a mouse in the folds of my jacket," he pointed out.

Fiona knew she had to talk hard, and fast. "The only thing wrong with this mouse is that he's not where you want him to be. So all we have to do is put him where he can get by without bothering us." The gnawing inside the box sounded busier. "Soon."

"Fiona," her father said, "try not to make your mother any more nervous."

Make *her* nervous, Fiona thought. Here I am, alone in the backseat, with a mouse about to climb out in my lap any minute.

"Personally," she said, "I think you should admire anything so determined to get out of a box, when outside is so huge and scary."

Her mother slowed the car. "Fiona, I am trying to think of a place to let him go."

"The park," Mr. Foster said.

Fiona was so relieved her nose felt stuffy, as if she had to cry. But she was not going to take chances with this mouse's life. "Not the park. It's full of dogs and joggers."

"Fiona, what do you want?" Her father's voice was controlled, but barely. "You want us to find a condominium that welcomes rodents?"

The gnawing seemed louder, and Fiona expected to see a mouse nose poke through any second. "Mama," she said, talking as rapidly as she could without stumbling over her words, "you remember that time we were taking a lot of junk to the dump, and we got lost? We drove down that dirt road until it ended, and then we had to back out. Remember, we could hear water."

"You expect me to drive down that same miserable road and then *back out* again and risk getting stuck?" her mother asked.

"Yes. Yes, I do. You're a good driver, and you're basically a good person, and you care about how I feel."

"Fiona," her father said wearily, "if you ever go into politics, remind me to be on your side."

It was no more than fifteen minutes to the field, but it was the longest ride Fiona had ever endured. She sat holding down the box lid. The mouse was gnawing near the bottom of the box, but holding the lid gave her something to do. She worried about his oxygen supply, but she knew that she dared not borrow a pencil or a pen from her father to make a little airhole. She was very, very sure she had pushed her parents as far as they could be moved. Besides, what if she poked the mouse? A mere poke with a pen could be a serious injury to something so small.

At last Mrs. Foster turned off onto a dirt road. The car jounced along amid a forest of weeds, until there was no more road, only weeds ahead. Then they stopped.

Fiona opened her door and climbed out carefully.

"Here?" Mr. Foster got out too.

"Where the water is," Fiona said.

She made her way through the weeds, her parents following. The sun was low, turning red in a last blaze. The day's heat was just beginning to ease. They seemed cut off from the world in that field. The only sounds were their moving through the brush, the enveloping hum of bugs finishing up the day, and the steady gnawing of the mouse.

When Fiona heard the other sound, barely louder than the bugs and the mouse, she stopped.

The weeds around her feet were green, and a tiny rill of a stream threaded among them.

"It's not much. But it's enough." She set the box beside the water, lifted off the lid, and stepped back.

Whisk! The mouse scrambled out and streaked in amid the brush.

Mrs. Foster put a hand on Fiona's arm. "Let's get out of here. He needs to be alone."

As they walked back to the car, Fiona reached for her mother's hand. "What are stocks?"

"Stalks?" Mrs. Foster asked.

"Stocks. Country mice eat stocks."

"*Stocks,*" Mr. Foster said. "They're a kind of plant."

"Are there any around here?" Fiona asked.

"A field like this is a smorgasbord of things that mice eat," Mr. Foster assured her.

Fiona reached to take his hand. She knew she was at an age where she looked silly walking between her parents and holding their hands, but there was nobody around to see them.

"I would keep you," she said. "If I had a choice of anybody rich or famous or you guys, I'd still stick with you."

They stopped at a deli on the way home, and ate in their family room so Mrs. Foster could put her feet up.

After dinner, Mr. Foster took Fiona back to the mall.

It was nothing like shopping with her mother. Fiona had to pick out her own blouses and sweaters and skirts. Her father said each of them looked fine, and he didn't understand why she even bothered trying them on. Nor did he understand about socks matching sweaters and skirts. He said white socks would go with everything.

He stayed calm and agreeable all through their shopping.

Fiona came home with two of the skirts she'd tried on with her mother, some blouses and sweaters and white socks and underwear, but no coat. When you buy a coat you need to be with somebody who gets *involved*.

On the first day of school, Fiona wore a skirt and blouse and sweater, white socks, and the shoes like Pauline's. She knew that if she tried to wear any other shoes, her mother would make her change, and by then Pauline and Barbara might have started for school.

Fiona hurried through breakfast, and picked up the bag lunch her mother had fixed. She was unsure about carrying a bag lunch, but it was safer until she knew how to go about buying lunch. At least she didn't have to carry a babyish lunch box.

"Well, I'll see you." Suddenly, she was scared to leave.

"Fiona, it's barely seven-thirty," her mother protested.

"I want to be sure Pauline and Barbara don't forget about me and start early."

91

"You sure you don't want me to drive you?" Mr. Foster asked.

"That's okay, thank you." Fiona could imagine nothing more embarrassing than having your father drive you to the first day of school, especially when you were wearing dumb shoes.

The morning was cool and clear. Fiona ran all the way to Pauline's.

She knocked on the front door, wondering what she would do if Mrs. Cahill opened it and said, "Oh, Pauline left ages ago."

Mrs. Cahill opened the door. "Fiona Foster, what in the world are you doing here at this hour? Now Pauline will feel rushed and wolf her breakfast. After this, you come at a reasonable time."

Mrs. Cahill shut the door. Fiona sat on the porch steps. About the time she began to wonder if Pauline had forgotten her and left by the back door, the front door opened.

Fiona was relieved to see that Pauline was dressed almost the same as she, even to the shoes.

"They made me carry a lunch box," Pauline said as they walked down the steps. "They said the cafeteria might not be open. You want to trade lunches?"

Fiona gripped the top of the paper bag. "I'd better not."

When they got to Barbara's, Mrs. Lawson opened the door in her bathrobe. "Barbara's not quite ready," she said, and shut the door.

"You notice that parents never ask you in?" Pauline asked as they sat on the steps. "If somebody comes to our house to ride to work with my dad, do you think my mother makes him wait on the porch?"

Howard and Larry came down the street wearing new clothes and carrying lunch boxes.

How did they all know? Fiona wondered. She hadn't heard Howard or Larry or Barbara or Pauline say a word to one another about walking to school together.

Then she realized they didn't have to. They'd known one another so long, they probably had been walking to school together for years.

Barbara came out wearing a plaid skirt and a blouse and sweater, and faded sneakers.

"Where's your lunch?" Howard asked her.

"I'm buying." Barbara walked down the porch steps.

"My folks weren't sure the cafeteria would be open," Larry said.

"If it isn't, you guys can share yours."

The five of them walked to the corner.

Pauline looked down at Barbara's sneakers. "What happened to your new shoes?"

"I wore them to my grandmother's yesterday and got a blister."

"You *lucky!*" Pauline was fervent.

"You know you can get blood poisoning from a blister?" Larry asked.

"You sound just like my grandmother," Barbara said.

He stopped and faced her. "Yeah? Well, it's true."

93

"If you got blood poisoning, would your mother ever feel guilty she made you buy those shoes!" Pauline said.

Barbara considered for only a second. "It wouldn't be worth it, if I had to have my foot cut off."

There looked to be hundreds of people in front of the school when they arrived. Fiona felt a little nervous, but being with friends helped.

Besides, at least a third of the girls whose feet Fiona could see were wearing the same dumb shoes as hers.

6

"I have to go to the dentist today," Fiona said one Monday in the cafeteria, in case anybody had been planning to ask her to play baseball after school.

In all the months since she'd moved to town, nobody had ever asked her to play baseball.

"Trade you my corn chips for your pickles," Howard said to Larry.

". . . so I won't be around," Fiona went on.

"Oh, no!" Pauline peeled back the top slice of bread on her sandwich. "Yellow mustard! My mother knows I *hate* yellow mustard!"

". . . in case anybody wants to know," Fiona added, beginning to feel irritated.

"Who wants my cupcake?" Larry added.

Barbara squinted at it. "Eeyew! It's *apple*. An apple cupcake!"

Fiona got up and stomped away.

At the end of the school day, Fiona left the building with Howard and Larry and Barbara and Pauline.

"So listen," Fiona said, "I don't know how long I'll be at the dentist's. Maybe all afternoon."

"Pollard?" Barbara asked her.

"How did you know?" Fiona asked.

"Everybody goes to Dr. Pollard. She's the only children's dentist in town."

"Pauline's got to be on my team this time," Fiona heard Howard say to Larry. "You had her last time."

Howard and Barbara and Larry and Pauline raced down the front bank to the sidewalk.

Fiona walked down the stairs, telling herself they were probably all terrible ball players.

Her family's station wagon was parked behind a school bus. Since it was a clear day, there were only a few parents waiting in cars.

All the cars were newer and shinier than the Fosters'.

Fiona got in beside her mother. As they pulled away from the curb, the engine made a clunking sound.

"The first dentist in this town to keep evening hours is going to make a fortune," Mrs. Foster said. "I don't know how they expect working people to take off at three."

"I could have gone by myself," Fiona said.

"For your first check-up with a new dentist? What kind of a person would she think I was?"

"A working person."

Mrs. Foster drove a dozen blocks to a new two-story building. In the parking lot were raised sections planted with ivy and young trees.

The dental offices were on the first floor. On a wide door that looked like carved wood were the gold letters EDNA W POLLARD, DDS; and under them, LUTHER STONE, DDS.

The waiting room was big, with dark-blue carpets, a blue sofa, and three chairs upholstered in real cloth. There was a coffee table in front of the sofa, and end tables by the chairs. In one corner was a fish tank. In another corner was a low table with picture books on it and three little chairs around it. A boy who looked about two years old lay under the table, kicking it.

Mrs. Foster steered Fiona to a partition with a window in it and waited until the receptionist slid back the glass.

"Fiona Foster to see Dr. Pollard," Mrs. Foster announced.

The receptionist smiled without looking above Mrs. Foster's nose. "Doctor's running a little late. Would you just have a seat and fill out this patient information sheet for Fiona?" She handed Mrs. Foster two sheets of paper on a clipboard and slid the window shut.

Fiona sat on the sofa beside her mother, careful not to look at the little boy. It wouldn't do to attract his attention. Most kids weren't even tame before five. She got up and looked through the magazines in the rack, but she wasn't really interested in *Money* or *Good Housekeeping*.

A nurse opened a door to the inner rooms and called out "Philip?"

The boy got up from under the table and went to her.

Fiona wandered over to the fish tank near the sofa. It was a handsome, clear-glass tank, taller than it was wide, and six sided, so it looked like an enormous jewel. Its water bubbled softly, and its green plants were real, not plastic. As the water bubbled, they swayed.

So did the fish.

That was about all he could do.

He was not a flashy fish, but he was a pleasant blue-gray, with cream-colored speckles.

Being nearly as long as the tank was wide, he couldn't swim more than a few inches without bumping the tank wall.

"That's a big fish," Fiona told her mother.

Mrs. Foster looked up. "It certainly is."

"It's a small tank."

"It looks big to me."

"It would be a big tank for a small fish," Fiona said. "For a big fish, it's a small tank.'"

Mrs. Foster went back to filling out the form.

Fiona watched the fish.

Her mother returned the form to the receptionist, then took a magazine from the rack and sat on the sofa again.

"I wonder how long he's been in it?" Fiona asked.

Her mother looked up from the magazine. "Who? What?"

"The fish. In the tank. I wonder if he ever lived in a lake or a stream. I wonder if they put him in the tank so long ago that nobody notices how he's outgrown it."

"I have no idea." Mrs. Foster turned a page.

"It's sure no kind of a life," Fiona observed.

Her mother looked up again. "What?"

"Just hanging there in the water."

"I could not even guess how much exercise a fish requires," Mrs. Foster sounded a little weary.

"It's not *requiring*," Fiona said. "It's that fish swim, and this one can't."

The nurse opened the door from the inner offices and said, "Fiona?"

Mrs. Foster stayed where she was as Fiona followed the nurse. They had both been through enough checkups to know that dentists didn't welcome parents in the examination room.

The room this nurse took Fiona to was all pink, even to the chair and the machinery. The nurse put Fiona in the chair and fastened a pink paper bib around her neck and moved a tray beside her. Then she left Fiona to gaze at the instruments on the tray.

By now, of course, Fiona knew that dentists didn't hurt. Even so, the instruments looked faintly sinister.

A short young woman with brown eyes and curly red hair came around the chair and stood by the tray. "Fiona? I'm Dr. Pollard. How are you?"

Fiona knew this would be a logical time to mention that the fish was too big for his tank.

Before she could speak, Dr. Pollard said, "Would you open up for me?"

Dr. Pollard peered into Fiona's mouth with mirrors and poked with instruments. "Do you brush after every meal and at bedtime?"

Fiona tried to say, "Oh, yes," but with the dentist's hand in her mouth, it came out sounding like a gargle.

As soon as she could speak properly, Fiona thought, she would bring up the fish. It's not often you have to tell a person you've just met that she is mistreating her fish. It would have to be said carefully and politely.

Dr. Pollard poked around Fiona's gums with a metal hook. "Do you know how to use floss?"

Hoping the dentist had a steady hand, Fiona made another gargling *yes* noise.

"Fine." Dr. Pollard took her hand out of Fiona's mouth. "Now, we're going to take a couple of pictures," Before Fiona could speak, she left the room.

A nurse stuck film in a cardboard holder in one side of Fiona's mouth, left the room and pressed the x-ray button, then returned and took the film and holder out. She did the same thing with film in the other side

100

of Fiona's mouth, and left after she took the film out.

Fiona practiced in her mind how she would bring up the matter of the fish.

"Fiona's doing pretty well." Dr. Pollard came around to the side of the chair, followed this time by Mrs. Foster. "She could brush a little more carefully." Dr. Pollard stuck the little x-ray films on a lighted wall panel. "She has two tiny cavities. See that little shadow there?"

Mrs. Foster bent close to the panel, squinting.

"And here." The dentist pointed with a pencil. "We'll take care of those. Then we'll have Fiona come back to have her teeth cleaned and her fillings polished."

If my teeth didn't happen to be in my mouth, Fiona thought, they wouldn't even need me in here, for all the attention they pay me.

Fiona had a lot on her mind that evening. "When somebody asks 'How are you?' why are you supposed to say 'Fine' even when you're not?"

"You don't want to bore people with your troubles." Mrs. Foster looked suspiciously into the salad bowl. "Burt, did you use the low-calorie dressing?"

"What if you're not fine?" Fiona asked. "What if you're worried?"

"I used the oil-free," her father said. "Isn't that the same as low-calorie?"

"I'm worried about my dentist's fish," Fiona said.

Her father looked at her mother. "She's what?"

101

"She's worried about the fish in the dentist's waiting room."

Mr. Foster put his fork down. *"Why?"*

"Because he's a big fish in a small tank," Fiona told him.

"She thinks the tank is too small for the fish," her mother translated.

"I wanted to tell Dr. Pollard, but she wouldn't pay attention."

Fiona's parents looked at each other silently. She could see by the looks that they were worried about her, not the fish. She suspected they would talk about her as soon as she went to bed. But they were not going to do anything for the fish.

Fiona got to Pauline's house the next morning a moment ahead of Howard and Larry. Barbara was just coming down the porch steps.

"Pauline's staying home," she told them. "She has the sniffles."

"She's so lucky," Howard marveled. "She always gets sniffles that go away by Saturday."

"You know that fish in Dr. Pollard's waiting room?" Fiona asked Barbara as they walked on. "That big fish?"

"You think that fish is big?" Barbara demanded. "My grandmother has a bunch of fish in a pond at her place that are twice that size."

"But they're in a pond," Fiona pointed out. "Dr. Pollard's fish is in that little tank."

"That's why my grandmother's fish are so big. Her pond is huge."

Larry slowed down. "What do you mean? You mean that if a goldfish grows up in the ocean, it's going to get as big as a whale?"

"A whale," Barbara told him coldly, "is not a fish."

"Maybe if you mentioned to Dr. Pollard . . ." Fiona began, but Larry interrupted.

"A whale is not a fish? So what is it? A bird? A person?"

Barbara looked at him as if he were something spilled on the sidewalk. "A whale is a . . . a . . . a thing like we are."

"A mammal," Howard said. "Whales are mammals. So are humans."

Fiona kept in step with Barbara. "I think it would help if somebody besides me also mentioned to Dr. Pollard—"

"*Sure*," Larry said. "You always see whales driving around town, playing basketball—"

"Ask your teacher." Howard was calm. "Ask in the library."

"Ask your neighborhood whale," Larry said.

Barbara stopped. "Okay, you want to bet? When you lose, I get to pitch the next game."

"That's not fair," Larry protested. "If you pitch, our whole team loses."

"A whale is not stuck in a fish tank he can't even swim around in!" Fiona exploded.

Larry and Howard and Barbara stopped walking and stared at her, astonished.

Fiona strode on, not even waiting for them to catch up.

When she got out of school that afternoon, her family station wagon was parked behind a school bus.

Her father leaned over to open the door. "Your mother called me. Your dentist had a cancellation, so you got lucky."

Fiona didn't even try to pretend she was amused.

As soon as her father gave her name to the receptionist, Fiona led him across the waiting room to the fish tank. "See what I mean?"

"It's a handsome fish," he said. "Listen, honey, I have to run to the bank for a minute. I should be back before you're finished."

Fiona didn't even watch him go. Okay, she thought, so nobody cares about this fish. All this fish has is me.

She stood by the tank, thinking of what she would say and how she would say it.

Finally, she made herself walk to the receptionist's window.

When it slid open, Fiona said, "Well." She was careful to be polite. "I see you still have that fish in that tank."

"We do." The receptionist looked over Fiona's head at a woman who had just come in. "May I help you?"

Fiona went back to sit on the sofa. She tried to think of something that would be courteous, but still make it clear that the fish had a serious problem.

It was harder to walk to the window a second time.

The receptionist took longer to slide it open.

"The thing is," Fiona said, "it's sad to see a big fish in a small tank. I mean, think how he must feel in there."

The receptionist smiled. "Oh, honey, fish don't feel anything." She shut the window.

Fiona went back to watch the fish. You don't yell at grown-ups, especially not people who work with your dentist.

The nurse she'd seen before called Fiona in and showed her to a room with blue walls, blue cabinets, and a blue chair.

Fiona's mind was so full of the fish, she didn't even worry about having her teeth filled.

A few minutes after the nurse left, Dr. Pollard came in. She stood by the tray, smiling and smelling of cinnamon mouthwash. "How are you today, Fiona?"

Fiona made herself speak very firmly. "Worried."

Dr. Pollard put a cool, scrubbed hand on her arm. "Fiona, I'm just going to do two tiny fillings."

"I'm worried about the fish in your waiting room. His tank is so small he can't even swim around."

Dr. Pollard seemed taken aback. Then she grinned and shook her head. "Fiona, you are a card!" As the nurse came back in, Dr. Pollard said, "Fiona's worried about the fish in the waiting room."

The nurse chuckled. "Fiona, you are the limit."

Fiona sat with her mouth open and her mind working while her teeth were filled. There had to be a way to make people settle down and pay attention to the fish's miserable plight.

When the fillings were done, Dr. Pollard was cheerful. "That wasn't so bad, was it?"

"No." There's not much chance that anybody will take you seriously when your mouth is numb, Fiona knew.

"You go to the desk, and Ms. Lehman will tell you when to come back to have your teeth cleaned and your fillings polished," Dr. Pollard said.

Mr. Foster was sitting on the waiting room sofa, looking through a copy of *Money*. He stood. "All done?"

"We have to make an appointment to come back," Fiona said.

"We'll call when we get home." Mr. Foster headed for the door.

Am I the only person in the world who will even *think* about that fish? Fiona wondered.

She slumped as much as you can slump in a seat belt and shoulder harness, too downcast even to worry how her teeth would feel when the shot wore off.

They'd gone just a few blocks in the car when her father asked, "Are you all right?"

"How do you know fish can't feel anything?"

He looked surprised. "I didn't say fish can't feel anything."

106

"Dr. Pollard's receptionist did. How does she know?"

"Well . . ." Mr. Foster pondered as he drove. "Fish don't do much."

"They swim all the time if they can. If anybody catches them, they try like crazy to get away."

"They don't do anything useful, or creative."

"Neither does Oliver, but you don't see him crammed into a tiny tank."

Mr. Foster turned left at the corner, then left again at the next corner. He drove to the mall and parked in a reserved space under Molberry's. "Come on."

In spite of herself, Fiona was interested. Is he going to take me in for a treat to cheer me up? she wondered. Then she looked more closely at her father. No. No, he's not in a good mood, she decided. We're probably just going to get something he left at work.

Mr. Foster took Fiona up to the pet department on the second floor, and to the fish tanks at the back wall. "Pick any two goldfish. Pick any bowl. Just remember you have to clean the bowl and change the water weekly."

He just doesn't understand, Fiona thought. She tried to think of something to say, somewhere between flatly turning down the goldfish and taking them. She decided to get off the subject, but not too far.

"Do they change Dr. Pollard's fish's water weekly?"

Mr. Foster spoke very slowly, and very carefully. "That fish has an aquarium, with a filter and a motor to keep everything clean and fresh."

"How much would an aquarium cost?"

"Hundreds of dollars." There was an edge to his voice now.

Fiona shook her head. "All that money, and the fish doesn't even have room to swim."

"Fiona, I do not want to hear another word about Dr. Pollard's fish! You want a goldfish or not?"

Fiona could see her father was getting annoyed. While she didn't want to make his mood worse, she couldn't lie. "I don't think so," she said politely. "It would only keep reminding me of . . . you know."

Mr. Foster strode out of the pet department so fast Fiona had to run to keep up with him.

He didn't speak all the way home.

Mrs. Foster greeted them in the entry hall. "Let me see your fillings."

"We have to call for an appointment to get them polished." Fiona opened her mouth.

Her father went back to the family room.

"I think maybe you'd better call for the appointment," Fiona told her mother.

That evening, after Fiona finished her homework, she laid her crayons out on the floor and set aside everything but the blues and greens and grays and cream. It's up to me now, she thought. She went down to the family room. "Do you have any kind of cardboard I could use to make a poster?"

Mrs. Foster put down the newspaper. "When is it due?"

"The sooner the better."

Mrs. Foster stood up, looking stern. "After this, you don't wait until the last minute to ask for help with a project."

After half an hour or so, her mother brought a big white gift box, flattened out, to Fiona's room. "Would this do?"

"Oh, yes. Thanks." Fiona hurried to take it. "When is Be Kind to Animals Week?"

"Sometime in May, I think. Why?"

Fiona had hoped it would be sooner. "Are you sure?"

"It sounds like a sensible month."

From downstairs, Mr. Foster called, "Where's the *TV Guide*?"

"You're probably sitting on it," Mrs. Foster shouted, and went back downstairs.

Fiona sat down with the box.

At the top of the cardboard, in big navy-blue capitals, she printed

BE KIND TO ANIMALS

Under that she drew a picture of a fish tank, with a large, speckled, gray-green fish almost filling it.

Fiona could remember making posters for Be Kind to Animals Week at her last school, but that was a long time ago. She remembered seeing Be Kind to Animals Week posters at the library where she used to live. As she recalled, they had pictures of puppies and kittens and captions like

BE GENTLE TO YOUR CAT

or

DON'T LET YOUR DOG RUN LOOSE

The best Fiona could come up with now was

FISH NEED SPACE, TOO

After she finished the poster, she slid it under her
bed so it wouldn't get stepped on.

7

The next morning Fiona finished her breakfast in a hurry and kissed her parents good-bye.

Her father looked surprised. "You don't have to leave for another ten minutes."

"I need to be early today," she said.

She got her poster from under her bed and hurried out the front door while her parents were still having coffee. There was no sense reminding her father of fish before he'd finished eating.

She carried the cardboard with the picture side toward her.

Fiona had yet to work up the courage to face Barbara's parents, and Pauline still had the sniffles. There

111

would have been no time to wait around for them, anyway.

It was important to get to school early with the poster. Mr. Langhorn, her teacher, might be a little confused having somebody bring a Be Kind to Animals Week poster a few months early.

That will be my chance to explain about the fish to him, she thought. If he has any heart, he'll even help me put it up on the wall where nobody in the room can miss it. And then I'll explain it for Show and Tell.

Since Dr. Pollard is the only children's dentist in town, some of the people in the class have to be patients of hers. One kid, *one* kid, she and her nurses and receptionist can ignore. But when a lot of kids mention that they saw her fish on their classroom wall, she'll have to pay attention.

What with keeping the picture close to her and struggling to hang on to her books and lunch bag, Fiona was not able to walk nearly as fast as she'd expected.

Other kids, even some who looked no bigger than first graders, were passing her.

"Yo! Fiona!" somebody behind her called.

"Fiona! Wait up!"

Howard and Larry ran up on her right and Barbara on her left.

"What have you got?" Larry asked.

"It's for school." Fiona kept walking. There was no sense standing on the sidewalk explaining a poster.

"Come on." Barbara stepped in front of her. "What is it?"

Knowing that Barbara would not move, or give up, until she saw the poster, Fiona stopped and turned it around.

Howard and Barbara and Larry studied it.

"Fiona," Barbara said sincerely, "you are really a weird person."

Fiona handed Larry her lunch bag and gave Howard her books. Nobody said another word about the poster.

As they got near school, the sidewalk was crowded.

Walking up the school's front stairs, Fiona held her poster closer. At the top, two boys from her room, Noel Gibson and Alan Drew, grabbed at it.

"Whatcha got? Whatcha got?" Alan demanded.

"It's a fish poster," Barbara told him sternly.

"*Fish* poster?" Before Fiona could move, Noel snatched it from her.

"Give it back!" Larry ran after him.

As Alan started after them, Barbara pinned his arms behind him.

Howard raced across the grass after Larry and Noel. Three of Noel's friends from their class joined the chase.

"*Okay! That's about it!*" Fiona had never felt such outrage.

She dashed through the gang of Noel's friends without even slowing down, and caught up to Larry and Noel.

"Fight! Fight!" she heard somebody yell.

Larry was trying to pull the poster away from Noel. Any second, Fiona knew, it would rip.

She grabbed Noel by the shoulders and yanked. At the same instant, her feet slid on the grass, and she fell.

Hauled right off his feet, Noel hung on to the poster . . . or to the part left in his hands. As he twisted to get free of Fiona, they rolled down the grass embankment.

Neither of them made a sound.

Fiona kept her right hand gripped around Noel's left ear and her left hand in his hair, even when they hit the sidewalk.

The concrete was hard and rough, but she hung on, not even caring that there was a crowd around her.

Then somebody in the crowd gasped, "Mr. Elliot!"

Fiona let go of Noel. Scrambling to his feet, Noel ran.

Fiona stood, feeling as if she must have left great patches of her skin on the sidewalk.

She saw Mr. Elliot catch Noel by the library and haul him away by the collar.

Bending, Fiona picked up the piece of poster. It was wet and covered with grass stains, and almost all the writing and picture had been scraped off.

Still too furious to worry about the people staring at her, she trudged up to the girls' bathroom. The bathroom was empty, and nobody followed her in.

All that work for nothing, she thought, as she ripped the piece of poster into smaller bits and threw them into the trash can. Nobody listens, nobody cares, and when I try to do something, this is how it ends up. It's not fair. It's not fair and it's not *right*!

Wincing, she dabbed at her scrapes with a wet paper towel and washed the grass stains off her skin. It hurt, but she was too outraged to feel the sting all that much.

As she came out of the bathroom, she saw Howard and Larry, herded by Ms. Bristow, one of the fourth-grade teachers. Larry's shirt was torn and he had a bump on his cheekbone. The knees of Howard's jeans were scuffed through, and the heels of his hands were bleeding.

Howard handed Fiona another piece of poster. "It got kind of wrecked."

"We have to go to the principal's office," Larry said.

"They nailed Barbara, too," Howard added. "She emptied out Alan's lunch box and stomped his corn chips right into the ground."

They ignore me, they drive me crazy, Fiona thought, but when it comes right down to it, they're my friends.

Ms. Bristow tightened her grip on Larry and Howard's shoulders. "Come along."

"They didn't start it," Fiona protested.

"They finished it." While Ms. Bristow was not large, she was scary.

"They were trying to rescue my poster," Fiona explained.

"Well, you have it," Ms. Bristow said. "Go to your class."

"Go on," Larry urged Fiona. "If you come and blame the other guys, everybody will call us a bunch of finks."

Ms. Bristow marched him and Howard toward the office.

The bell rang. Fiona stuffed the piece of paper into a trash can in the hall and hurried to her room.

Mr. Langhorn, her teacher, was still taking roll when a gym teacher brought Noel and Alan into the room. Alan clutched his lunch box, which was dented and missing its handle. One of his sweater sleeves had been pulled out of shape, so he seemed to be walking lopsided. Noel's eyes looked puffy, and his left ear was red.

They stood quietly, except for Noel's sniffling, while the gym teacher talked to Mr. Langhorn in a low voice.

When the gym teacher left, Mr. Langhorn fixed Alan and Noel with a hard stare. "Take your seats. You will stay in the room for every recess, and you will not speak unless I call on you. Is that clear?" Without waiting for an answer, he went on with the roll call.

Fiona's relief was mixed with just a scrap of guilt. I'm the only one who got away with it, she thought. Mr. Elliot was so busy chasing Noel, he didn't even get a good look at me.

And Noel didn't fink on me. I'm the only one who's

not in trouble because Noel didn't fink. In spite of herself, Fiona felt a little bit of respect for Noel.

Alan and Noel shuffled to their seats. As they passed Fiona, Noel whispered, *"Fish heads."*

A thing like that catches on. Several people had seen the scuffle and the poster. At recess, Fiona was followed by half a dozen classmates whispering, "Fish heads."

She knew that if she chased them, they'd scatter. And she was pretty sure the assistant principal and the gym teacher and Ms. Bristow had her under suspicion already.

The thing to do is ignore all the whispers, she decided.

It was not easy.

At lunch Barbara and Howard and Larry had to sit at a table with Alan and Noel and four teachers. Fiona found an empty table. Three people sat down at the other end and stared at her, muttering, "Fish heads." One of them wasn't even in her class.

Tempted as she was to scramble right over the table at them, Fiona reminded herself that all she had gotten from tackling Noel were scrapes and grass stains and half a ruined poster.

And this time there were four teachers probably just waiting for her to make a move.

At afternoon recess she had a dozen people following her around the school yard, chanting, "Fish heads! Fish heads!"

Terrible as the day was, Fiona was not tempted to complain. They won't make me cry, she told herself, and they'll never make me fink. But I have taken all I'm going to take. From *anybody*.

At the final bell she waited in her seat until everybody but the teacher had left. When she finally walked out of the room, Howard and Larry and Barbara were waiting in the hall.

They walked down the corridor, chants of "Fish heads!" all around them.

"We would be in big trouble if we took after them," Barbara muttered through her teeth.

"But it will be worth it," Fiona said.

She stopped and bent over the water fountain, waiting for her tormentors to come close enough to catch.

"Fish heads!" Darting in suddenly, somebody shoved Larry into her.

The sound of her front tooth hitting the fountain shocked Fiona even before she felt the pain. Straightening up, she touched her lip, then looked at her fingers. Seeing the blood, she felt dizzy for a second, and then she hurt so much she sat down, right there in the hall.

The noise around her stopped. The people around her looked scared and then hurried away, except for Barbara and Larry and Howard.

Barbara's voice was awed. "You've got blood all over your blouse!"

"You want to go to the office?" Larry asked.

Fiona shook her head.

"You're lips are turning all blue." Howard's voice was shaky.

"I want to go home," Fiona said.

Larry and Howard carried her books, and Barbara held her under the elbow almost all the way home. Three houses before Fiona's, Barbara let go of her and ran ahead, yelling, *"Mrs. Foster! Fiona's been wounded!"*

Mrs. Foster came running out the front door and raced to Fiona.

"Oh, my word. Oh, baby." She bent to look at Fiona's face. "Are you hurt anyplace else?"

Fiona shook her head and pointed at her front tooth.

Her mother took her in a taxi to the dentist. Barbara offered to come along, but Mrs. Foster thanked her and told her she'd already done enough.

Ms. Lehman, the receptionist, slid back the glass and looked at Fiona. "Oh, my."

The nurse took Fiona in ahead of everybody in the waiting room. This time Mrs. Foster came along.

She held Fiona's hand even after Dr. Pollard came in.

Dr. Pollard looked at Fiona's mouth. "What happened?"

Though it hurt to talk, Fiona knew this was her chance. "I made a poster about how fish need room to swim. Some kids teased me about it, and I got my face banged on the fountain." Fiona went on, before anybody could tell her to keep her mouth open. "You know Barbara Lawson? Her grandmother has a huge pond. It'd be a great home for a fish."

"Open up," Dr. Pollard bent closer with a mirror.

"You're probably thinking a tank with no fish might look strange. But I'll tell you what I could do. I could get you a couple of goldfish."

"No more about fish," the dentist said. "It's been a long day."

She worked for a long time on Fiona's tooth. Finally she stood up and rubbed her back. "I've done all I can for now. I think I've saved it, but I want you to bring her back on Tuesday."

For breakfast the next morning Fiona had juice and a homemade shake. "I'll pack you some soup in a thermos," her mother said.

"My lip's all puffed out," Fiona murmured. "Couldn't I just stay home this morning?"

"That would just make it harder to go tomorrow morning," her father said.

"I've been through a lot, you know," Fiona told him.

Her father looked at her mother. "She has," he said. "She has been through a lot."

After Mr. Foster left for work, Mrs. Foster put Fiona back to bed, which Fiona found wonderfully silly.

"You want me to read to you?" Mrs. Foster asked.

"What about your deadline?"

"I always have deadlines. I have only one child."

120

There is nothing quite like having your mother cuddle in your bed and read you your favorite books. After *The Bat Poet* they had a few chapters of *Winnie-the-Pooh*, and then the best parts of *Through the Looking-Glass*.

"Now, we'll pretend this is a very, very fancy resort," Mrs. Foster said. "And you can phone for whatever you want for lunch."

"*Phone* down to our own kitchen?"

"Well, tell me. I'll relay it to the cooks."

"*Anything* I want?"

"Anything I can fix from whatever we have in the house. I'll even bring it on a tray."

Fiona almost grinned. "Nah. I'd only spill everything down my shirt."

She had lunch at the table with her mother—tomato soup with oyster crackers, juice with a straw, and three, *three* fruit bars.

"You realize," Mrs. Foster said, "this is not a completely balanced meal. If you weren't wounded, I'd have insisted you change your order a bit."

The day almost erased all the misery of the day before.

There was the next morning, though.

"What if everybody says, 'Fish heads,' at me all day?" Fiona worried when her father came in to wake her.

"They won't. They'll feel too guilty when they see you."

121

"You have a lot of faith in kids," Fiona said morosely.

Her father kissed her hair. "Mainly in my own. Why don't I drive you this morning?"

Ordinarily, of course, she would have refused, but this day she was grateful. She was pretty sure nobody would yell, "Fish heads," at a person getting out of her father's car.

Walking up the steps of the school, it was all she could do not to turn and run home. But everybody she encountered glanced at her uneasily, even respectfully.

Nobody bothered her in the halls. When she entered her room, Mr. Langhorn said, "Wow! What door did you walk into?"

Nobody else said a word.

Though it was a relief not to be teased, it was a lonely morning.

At recess, Barbara was waiting in the hall. "You look awful!" she said admiringly. "Are you going to lose your tooth?"

"I don't know. I have to go back to Dr. Pollard Tuesday at four thirty."

"If you lose it you can sue the kid who shoved Larry. You could even sue the school."

They wandered out to the playground. Howard and Larry hurried over to ask Fiona if she was going to lose her tooth, but everybody else left the four of them alone.

"When I told my mother what happened," Barbara

122

said, "she remembered Oliver and I were due for check-ups. I'll have her change our appointments to Tuesday."

"Why?"

"So we can hang out in the waiting room together."

Mrs. Lawson telephoned Fiona's mother that evening. "That should work out fine," Fiona's mother said when she hung up. "Barbara's mother will pick you all up from school and take you to the dentist if I'll bring you all home. That way I can meet you right there before your appointment."

Fiona had until Tuesday to worry about riding in a car with Mrs. Lawson. Certainly Barbara's mother wouldn't have forgotten the wedding, and Oliver and the beetle.

On the other hand, Fiona thought, if I'm in the waiting room with Barbara, I can *make* her look at the fish. Barbara wouldn't hesitate to speak up to anybody about anything. And Barbara is harder to ignore than I am.

On Tuesday afternoon Mrs. Lawson was waiting outside the school in her new silver sedan, Oliver strapped into the seat beside her.

Fiona climbed into the backseat with Barbara, wondering whether to say "Thank you for the ride," or just keep quiet.

Mrs. Lawson didn't speak until she'd driven several blocks. "When we get to the dentist's, you girls get right out of the car."

"I thought your meeting wasn't until four," Barbara said.

"The meeting is at four, but I'm not going to make it." Mrs. Lawson sounded tense. "Everything has gone wrong. Fiona's mother called; their car won't start, so I'll have to take you all home. And meanwhile, your father has locked himself in the upstairs bathroom. Don't ask how."

Even our car gets us into trouble with Barbara's parents, Fiona thought. And my mother won't even be there when Dr. Pollard decides what's going to happen to my tooth. Despite all that, Fiona could not help but be fascinated by the idea of a parent locking himself in a bathroom. She glanced at Barbara, hoping Barbara would dare to ask and maybe get an explanation. But Barbara, she saw, knew better than to speak.

At the next stop sign, Mrs. Lawson said, "He shut the bathroom door to paint it, and the lock stuck, and I can't find the little bathroom key. He's in there ranting that it's all my fault, and I do not want to hear another word on the subject. Is that clear?"

Even Oliver sat motionless.

Mrs. Lawson pulled into the dentists' parking lot. "I'm going to have to rush to the hardware store. I'll get one of those little key things, if they still make them, and then dash home and let him out, and we are not going to discuss it any further. All right?"

She unstrapped Oliver and hoisted him out of his

car seat and stood him on the pavement. Then she took hold of his wrist and hurried toward the building. Oliver didn't even have a chance to decide whether he *wanted* to run.

Barbara and Fiona followed them into the dentists' waiting room. When Ms. Lehman opened the glass, Mrs. Lawson said, "Barbara and Oliver Lawson for checkups and Fiona Foster for something. Do you mind terribly if I leave them and come back? I have an emergency at home."

"Oh, heavens no!" Ms. Lehman assured her. "You run along!"

The waiting room was full, with four adults and a little girl who sat on the low table with her shoes off, her eyes shut, and a book over her head.

"Keep Oliver out of trouble and out of the way," Mrs. Lawson instructed Barbara, and rushed out of the waiting room.

As Oliver started after his mother, Barbara grabbed his hand.

Oliver's face got red. He opened his mouth and squeezed his eyes shut.

"Hey, you want to see the fish?" Barbara led him to the tank.

Fiona followed. "I thought when somebody got locked in a bathroom, you could call the fire department."

"The *upstairs* bathroom?" Barbara's voice was hushed but fierce. "Can you picture it if my mother called the fire department? Red trucks and sirens, and

125

firefighters climbing up a ladder to our *bathroom* and hauling my father out the window in front of the whole neighborhood? My father runs a *bank!*"

Oliver gazed at the fish.

"Look at that," Fiona said to Barbara. "Look at the size of the fish and the size of the tank. Can you imagine how he feels?"

"How would I know how a fish feels?" Barbara growled.

"That's just it. You don't know, so you should be especially careful how you treat them. I told Dr. Pollard about your grandmother's pond, but she didn't want to listen. You tell her the pond would be a perfect home for this fish."

"Listen," Barbara said firmly, "When a dentist has my teeth in her hands, I'm not saying anything she doesn't want to hear."

Ms. Lehman slid open the glass. "Is this Oliver's first checkup?" she asked Barbara.

"I guess so," Barbara said.

"Could you answer a few questions for us?"

"Watch Oliver," Barbara told Fiona, and strolled to the window.

Fiona held Oliver's hand and watched the fish. He hung in the water, barely moving his fins.

"Poor fish," Fiona said.

Oliver stared into the tank. "Poor fish."

Fiona was astonished. She had never heard him speak before.

The little girl on the table opened her eyes, let the book fall off her head, and came over to the tank.

"Poor fish!" Oliver's voice was loud, and surprisingly deep.

A woman sitting on the sofa glanced at him uneasily.

"*Poor fish!*" Oliver boomed.

The woman got up and went to stand by the magazine rack.

"I never heard Oliver talk before!" Fiona said as Barbara came back.

Barbara was grim. "Neither has anybody else."

A man came in with a boy of about three. While the man spoke to Ms. Lehman, the boy stood quietly beside him.

"Poor fish," Oliver crooned.

"How do you do it?" Barbara asked Fiona. "How do you do these things to him? Parents are supposed to be around when a kid says his first words. His first words are suppose to be 'Mama' or 'Daddy' or even 'Bye-bye,' not 'Poor fish.' And he's not supposed to say them in front of a bunch of strangers in a dentists' waiting room."

"Poor fish." The little girl who'd come over to the tank peered at the fish's face.

A man sitting on the sofa got up and went to stand by the receptionist's window.

"Miriam," a woman sitting on one of the chairs said to the little girl, "come over here and let Mama read you a story."

127

"Poor fish!" Miriam was as sincere as Oliver.

The boy who had just come in edged over toward them.

"If Dr. Pollard asks me how this happened," Barbara warned Fiona, "I'm not going to lie. I'll tell her you started it." She led Oliver over to the far wall.

Dr. Pollard's nurse opened the door from the inner offices. "Miriam?"

"Poor fish!" Miriam told her.

Miriam's mother strode to the tank, picked her up, and carted her in past the nurse.

The new boy regarded the tank solemnly. "Poor fish."

Fiona went to stand by Oliver.

A man came in with two little girls, one dressed in red corduroy, the other in blue velour.

The boy by the tank stroked the glass. "Poor fish. Oh, poor fish."

"Gregory," the man who'd brought him said, "come over here by Daddy."

The little girls who'd just entered stepped over to look at the fish, then at Gregory.

I could make a run for it, Fiona thought, but there is no place to run. I could hide in the bathroom, if I could find it. Then I would get into worse trouble than I've ever been in in my life. Even that would be nothing compared to facing Dr. Pollard now.

A nurse Fiona hadn't seen before came to the door. "Mrs. Yollin?"

"Here!" A woman got up from a chair and hurried to her.

Gregory pressed his nose to the tank. "Poor fish."

The little girl in red rested her forehead against the tank. "Poor fish."

"It's spreading!" Barbara hissed.

She was right. The little girl in blue said, "Poor fish," and then Gregory repeated it, and then the girl in red.

Gregory's father got him and sat him on a little chair by the low table.

"Poor fish," the little girl in blue called to Gregory.

"Poor fish," Gregory agreed.

The people in the chairs nearest the tank got up and stood around the room, looking at the carpet.

Dr. Pollard's nurse opened the door. Miriam came out with her mother.

"Oliver? Barbara?" The nurse looked tense.

Barbara led Oliver to her.

"Poor fish," Miriam said, passing them.

It was the most terrible time Fiona could remember since she'd brought her poster to school.

Terrible times, she realized, were occurring closer and closer together in her life.

At the same time, appalled as she was, she could not help being impressed at what she had set off. If she had not felt so scared, and so guilty, she would have found it exciting.

Just for a moment, she felt like a big sister . . . not

the Barbara kind . . . to the children chorusing "poor fish." For all their faults, there was some good in little kids. Nobody else had bothered to really look at the fish, or to care about him.

But I am going to pay for this, she thought. Boy, am I going to pay!

A woman came in with a boy of about seven. She gave his name to Ms. Lehman, who was looking more and more harried, and then glanced at the empty seats and the standing people.

Hesitantly, she sat on the sofa. To Fiona's relief the boy sat beside her, ignoring the tank.

The girl in red rested her cheek against the tank. "Poor fish."

"Poor, poor fish," echoed the girl in blue.

"*Oh, poor fish!*" Gregory cried.

"Shh!" Gregory's father hissed.

It was no use. The two little girls kept up the refrain, each sounding sadder and louder than the other.

The boy on the sofa looked at the woman beside him. "What's wrong with the fish?"

"I don't know, honey," she said.

He walked over to the tank. "What's wrong with the fish?" he asked the little girls.

Dr. Pollard will call my mother, Fiona thought. *She'll call my mother and tell her to come get me and never bring me back.*

"Poor fish," the little girls told the new boy, one after the other.

The boy walked over to the receptionist's window and rapped on the glass. Ms. Lehman opened it cautiously.

"There's something wrong with your fish," he told her.

The inner door opened and Barbara came out with Oliver. "Fiona?" the nurse called.

There was no way to escape, Fiona knew. She could say she was suddenly, desperately sick, but then they might call an ambulance.

"*Fiona*." The nurse looked right at her. "Come on in."

She led Fiona to the pink room, showed her to the chair, fastened a bib around her neck, and stalked away silently.

If this could just be a dream, Fiona thought, I would be willing to have an ordinary nightmare every week for the rest of my life.

She heard footsteps. Dr. Pollard came to the side of the chair and looked down at her. "Do you know two children have greeted me with 'Poor fish,' Fiona? When I pass near the waiting room, I heard a whole chorus of 'Poor fish.' "

"I only said it to Barbara!" Fiona blurted. "I didn't know it would catch on!"

"Open your mouth."

Sitting openmouthed, Fiona didn't dare look right at Dr. Pollard, and it was hard to look around her without seeming shifty eyed. Fiona looked at the ceiling poster, though it wasn't very interesting.

Dr. Pollard concentrated on her examination for a long time and then straightened up. "Where's your mother?"

"Home." If only she'd let me break it to Mama myself, Fiona thought.

"I'll call her."

Fiona was terrified, but she had to know. "What are you going to tell her?"

"That your tooth's all right."

Fiona waited in the chair, wondering miserably what else Dr. Pollard would tell her mother.

Finally Dr. Pollard came back. "Okay. Your mother says you're to go along with Mrs. Lawson."

My mother probably wouldn't even want to come get me, Fiona thought. She's heard all about it, and she'd be too ashamed to set foot in here.

"I'll see you for cleaning and for polishing those fillings," Dr. Pollard said.

Fiona was amazed. "You will?"

"Certainly." As Fiona slid out of the chair, Dr. Pollard added, "I told your friend Barbara that if her grandmother will take the fish, I'll throw in a year's fish food."

Fiona was stunned, not quite believing she had won. "I can buy you a couple of goldfish," she said hesitantly. "My father gets a discount."

"Oh, no. No. They would grow, and you'd make me send them to a pond. No, I'll plant ferns in the tank.

It should be years before they get so big you force me to send them to a good home in the forest."

As Fiona started out of the room, Dr. Pollard said, "Fiona."

Fiona turned. Here it comes, she thought. I should have known there'd be more.

"When you grow up and get busy, Fiona, sometimes you don't see important things anymore. Thank you for reminding me."

Grown-ups, Fiona thought. Grown-ups are strange and mysterious beings.

Mrs. Lawson was in the waiting room with Barbara and Oliver. There was a new child in the room, and a constant murmur of "Poor fish."

Leading Barbara and Fiona and Oliver to the parking lot Mrs. Lawson said, "I telephoned your mother a while ago, Fiona, and told her I was taking you all out to dinner."

"My father just got out of the bathroom so grumpy, my mother told him to eat by himself," Barbara explained.

"Never mind!" Mrs. Lawson put Oliver in his car seat and sorted out arms and legs and straps.

"Poor fish," he said.

"Good heavens!" His mother stood back. "Did you hear that?"

Barbara nodded.

"I know where he got it," Mrs. Lawson said. "He got it from that stupid game in the waiting room. You

133

can't control what they pick up from other children, but I am not going to write in his baby book that his first words were 'Poor fish.' "

Barbara got into the car. "Dr. Pollard is giving Grandma that big fish in her tank."

"She'll love it." Mrs. Lawson got behind the wheel. "Your father's mother would never turn down anything that was free."

"Also," Barbara pointed out, "she likes pets that don't shed."

"Poor fish," Oliver murmured.

"I guess a seafood restaurant is out," Barbara said, straight-faced.

Fiona didn't dare laugh out loud. She sat in the back-seat with Barbara, both of them struggling to control the giggles.

I may not be her best friend, Fiona thought, but she can be pretty neat sometimes.

8

"Why so quiet?" Fiona's father asked her.

Fiona stopped combing her fingers through the rug and sat up. "I was thinking."

"About what?"

"Pauline Cahill's big sister is getting married. Everybody I know has a sister who gets married."

"Everybody?"

"Barbara. Now Pauline."

"I saw the picture in the paper with the announcement," Mrs. Foster said. "Pauline's sister looked lovely."

Fiona went out to sit on the front porch so nobody would ask what else she was thinking. She knew her parents would only feel sad if they knew that she was thinking that, in all the months since they'd moved here, nobody had invited them to anything.

Barbara came up the walk, leading Oliver by the hand. In his padded jacket he looked like an advertisement for steel-belted radial tires.

"Do you know where everybody is?" Barbara asked. "Nobody's home, but they're not at the park."

Fiona shook her head.

Barbara sat on the step beside her. "You want to do something?"

"Like what?"

"I don't know. I asked you."

Fiona sat for a few minutes, and then asked, as if it didn't matter at all, "Are you going to Pauline's sister's wedding?"

"Sure."

"Will you be a flower girl?"

"Nah." Barbara grabbed a twig as Oliver tried to wedge his mouth open with it. "Pauline and her dumb cousin are."

Fiona decided to put the Cahill wedding out of her mind.

It's not easy, not thinking about the second wedding to which you're not going. Seeing Barbara and Pauline every day reminded Fiona. Even seeing Howard and Larry made her wonder if their parents had been invited. She couldn't ask them in front of Pauline.

As the days passed, Fiona grew more and more sure there was no chance of being asked. She told herself it was nothing new; she'd never been invited to a wedding.

The morning of the ceremony, she stopped telling herself anything.

"Could Pauline come to dinner next week?" she asked her mother.

"I suppose so," Mrs. Foster said.

Fiona went to her room and changed her clothes. While her parents were still in the kitchen, she called down. "Well, I guess I'll go over and tell Pauline she can come to dinner."

Fiona hurried out the front door. Seeing her dressed up, her parents might remember this was Pauline's sister's wedding day. They might say, "You can't go over there now. Remember Barbara's sister's wedding!"

Fiona had learned a lot from Barbara sister's wedding. This time she would simply go over to tell Pauline she was invited to dinner, and leave the rest up to her. If anybody *should* decide, on the spur of the moment, to say, "Why don't you stay for the wedding, Fiona?" it wouldn't hurt to be dressed for the occasion.

A few blocks from the Cahills', Fiona saw Howard prying his softball out of Spike's mouth. "Good dog," he told Spike, and wiped the slobbery ball on his jeans.

"Got a game?" Fiona asked, just in case they might be short a player.

Howard fell into step with her. "I have to find out

when Pauline will be finished with her sister's wedding. She's our only pitcher."

"Maybe one of you could pitch, and find somebody else to fill in."

"If anybody but Pauline pitches, all the other batters get to walk."

Fiona told herself that Howard and his friends had never asked her to play because they had grown up together. It had probably never occurred to them that anybody else might want to be on their team.

"Do you think it's going to be a big wedding?" Fiona asked, to get her mind off not being asked to play ball.

"I don't know," Howard said.

"Were your folks invited?"

"Who'd want to be invited to a wedding?"

They walked on. "What do you suppose people do if they're having a wedding and a lot of guests don't show up," Fiona wondered. "It would be embarrassing to have hardly anybody at a wedding."

"You'd have a lot of food left," Howard observed.

"I mean, you'd probably be ready to grab anybody who could come on short notice."

Half a block from the Cahills', Fiona saw that the sidewalk was jammed wth people heading for their front door.

"We'd better go around back so Spike doesn't jump on anybody," Howard said.

Fiona hesitated. "What if they're having the wedding out back?"

Howard looked at her as if she'd gone strange. "They wouldn't have an outdoor wedding in the *fall*. You think people wear coats and sweaters to a *wedding*?"

That made sense to Fiona. Though it was a pleasant, sunny day, there was no way to count on the weather in October. Still, she let Howard unlatch the gate and walk into the backyard ahead of her. If nobody yelled at Spike, she could be fairly sure no wedding was being held in the yard.

Nobody yelled.

Pauline was sitting on a swing, with Barbara standing by the side of the swing set holding Oliver's hand. They were all very clean. Barbara wore the flower-girl dress from her sister's wedding. Pauline had on a yellow dress with a full skirt and little cloth daisies all around the neck. Oliver wore a blue suit and white shirt.

"Our sitter got sick," Barbara announced. "I have to keep Oliver out here because my parents don't trust him not to yell 'Poor fish!' during the wedding."

Pauline brightened. "Hey, Fiona—"

Barbara looked worried. "I'm supposed to watch him."

"What's the difference?" Pauline asked. "Fiona could stay right here with him. Listen, Howard, Oliver threw his teddy in our front hedge. Will you get it for him?"

"When can you play ball?" Howard asked her.

"In a couple of hours." Pauline grabbed Barbara's arm. "Come on. I've got to get my flower-girl stuff."

So, dummy, Fiona told herself, you had to keep trying. And what did it get you? It got you left out here alone with Barbara's brother and Howard's dog.

Oliver tried to free his hand from hers. "Ba wa."

Fiona pretended not to notice he was struggling. "Uh . . . nice suit, Oliver."

"Ba wa!" He was more vehement.

"You mean bow wow?" She lifted him up to face Spike, who licked him from chin to brow.

Oliver scrunched up his face and drew a deep breath. "BA WA!"

"You mean water?" Fiona let him down and led him to the back door. She was uneasy about taking him into the house, but it was safer than letting him yell loud enough to wreck the wedding.

In the kitchen she stood him to one side of the swinging door, so it couldn't flatten him if anybody came in from the dining room. "Don't move, Oliver."

She climbed up on the counter and opened the cupboards, looking for a glass. When she found one, she slid off the counter and turned on the faucet. "Okay. Here we go."

There was no sound.

She turned.

She was alone in the kitchen.

"Oliver!" Fiona ran through the swinging door.

The long dining room table was set with a white damask cloth, tall white candles in silver holders, and silver trays piled with food.

140

On a small round table stood a four-tier wedding cake. Its white frosting was decorated with swirls and icing flowers and silvery candy pearls. On the very top stood a tiny bride and groom.

"Oliver?" Fiona bent down and lifted the cloth of the round table. She peered under the long table.

Then she opened the French doors and hurried into the side yard.

"Oliver! How did you get in here?" It was Barbara's voice, from the next room.

Fiona darted over to that room's window.

She was looking into a study. Pauline sat on a desk, while Barbara was scooping up Oliver. On the sofa were a big bouquet, two smaller ones, and two little baskets of flowers.

Howard came around from the front of the house carrying a teddy. "Yo, Oliver! Got your bear!" he called in the window.

Spike came bounding out the dining room's French doors. His nose was white, and candy pearls clung to the frosting on his whiskers.

"*Spike!*" Fiona cried.

She ran into the dining room.

One side of the bottom tier of wedding cake had been licked clean of frosting. A large piece was bitten out.

Howard stood outside the doors, holding Spike by the collar and looking as shaky as Fiona felt. "How did he get in there?"

Barbara and Pauline came running in from the hall. "What happened?" Barbara asked.

Fiona was too shocked to bluff. "I think I didn't shut the back door when I brought Oliver in."

Pauline looked at the cake, her face almost as pale as the remaining frosting. "There goes the wedding. There goes my whole life."

"Quick! Get the dog out of sight!" Barbara shut the French doors as Howard hustled Spike away. "I *told* you I should have stayed with Oliver!" she muttered at Pauline.

Pauline looked around her. "Oliver!"

They did not dare run through the hall now. Instead, they dashed out the French doors.

Through the study window they saw Oliver sitting on the rug, taking apart the bride's bouquet. Petals from the other bouquets and the flower baskets were scattered around him.

Barbara opened the window wider.

"They'll send me to boarding school," Pauline moaned, and climbed in the window after Barbara.

I've done it again, Fiona thought. The only sensible thing to do is go home. I wasn't even invited to this wedding.

On the other hand, the ruined cake and flowers were more or less her fault. She climbed in the window, as scared as she had been when facing Dr. Pollard.

Barbara snatched the bride's bouquet from Oliver

so fast he didn't even resist. "I'll hide this mess. You guys find more flowers."

"The parlor is full of them." Pauline's voice was shaky.

"It's full of people, too." Barbara shoved her and Fiona toward the window. "Get out there and grab anything growing."

Pauline and Fiona picked every bloom close to the house. They didn't dare venture farther into the yard and risk being spotted.

Tossing the flowers in the study window, they climbed over the sill again.

Barbara had given Oliver an appointment book to look at. Sitting on the floor, she and Fiona and Pauline began sticking the garden blossoms in among the tattered few left in the baskets and bouquets.

As Fiona shoved a red begonia into the center of what had been the bride's bouquet, she heard voices coming toward the study. Dropping the bouquet on the sofa, she dived for the window.

Barbara boosted Oliver over the sill to her, then climbed out, followed by Pauline.

As they squatted against the wall, they heard Pauline's sister wail, *"Mother! The flowers!"*

"Oh, I would sue that flower shop!" another woman exclaimed.

"They didn't look anything like that when they came." Mrs. Cahill sounded stunned.

"Mother, we can't use them!" Pauline's sister cried.

"It's too late now," Mrs. Cahill said. "Just . . . hold them close to you."

Barbara jerked her head toward the dining room doors and crept toward them, Pauline and Fiona after her. Oliver followed, thrilled by the game.

"What are you doing!" Pauline's aunt Maytrue towered over them. She was as tall and thin as a spear, elegant in a gray chiffon dress and long strings of beads. "You're going to ruin your clothes. Pauline, go get your flowers. The wedding's about to start." Aunt Maytrue hauled Fiona to her feet. "The rest of you get in here."

Barbara stood up. "I have to watch Oliver."

"And I'm not invited to—" Fiona began.

"Never mind about Oliver." Without releasing Fiona, the aunt took his hand from Barbara's. "Come along."

Most of the seats in the parlor were taken.

"Scoot over," Aunt Maytrue hissed at a man in the last row. Sitting on the sofa beside him, she nudged him even farther over with her elbow, took Oliver in her lap, and pulled Fiona down beside her.

Just let me out of here, Fiona thought. Just let me out of here, and I will never want to go to another wedding as long as I live.

But even if she could have freed herself from the aunt and slipped away unnoticed, she knew she wouldn't. Already she had ruined the day for the bride and her mother and attendants. And they hadn't even seen the wedding cake.

Fiona knew she and Barbara would have to get into the dining room and patch the cake before the ceremony ended. Maybe they could fill the hole the dog had made with cream cheese and then slather mayonnaise where the frosting had been.

No, she decided. A bitten, unfrosted wedding cake would be less of a shock than a cream-cheese-and-mayo one.

She jumped as a thin woman in a pink dress brought her hands down on the piano keys in a thundering chord.

As the woman played the wedding march, Pauline and her cousin walked in from the hall, carrying baskets with a few geraniums in them.

Clutching their bouquets like bottlenecks, trying to hold them together, the bridesmaids followed. They wore strained smiles, and their eyes kept darting down to the wobbly flowers they held.

Then came the bride and her father.

Wedged at the end of the sofa between Aunt Maytrue and Barbara, Fiona was at eye level with the bride's wild, strange, unsteady bouquet.

With a little whimper, Barbara grabbed Fiona's hand.

"Shh!" The aunt tweaked Barbara's sleeve.

Plump and fuzzy, striped brown and gold, a bee was crawling on the inside petals of the begonia in the center of the bride's bouquet.

Fiona's heart felt as if it were being squashed inside her chest. If I knew how, I should take my pulse, she thought. If my pulse is all funny, it means I am going to faint. Faint at a wedding where you're not supposed to be, and you're really in trouble. On the other hand, if I faint, somebody might open the doors for air, and the bee might get away.

She thought of the bee, outside, minding his business, when she'd plucked his begonia, thrown it into the study, and shoved it into a bouquet. This was one long-suffering bee. But the minute he was discovered in this room, there would be a panic. Some people went crazy with a bee around them. Once they started swatting at him, or throwing the bouquet around, he'd have every right to panic.

Whoever he stung would squash him like a bug. With Fiona's luck, it would be the bride.

Not even the cake was as important as saving the bee.

The wedding went on so long, Fiona wondered how the minister could keep standing, let alone talking. Now and then somebody coughed. Oliver snored softly on Aunt Maytrue's lap.

Finally, the bride and groom exchanged rings and kissed.

Pauline and her cousin walked back toward the entry hall, followed by the bridesmaids and the bride and groom.

"The cake!" Barbara whispered.

"You can just wait for cake." As Barbara scrambled off the couch, Aunt Maytrue grabbed Fiona's wrist.

The aunt's grip was like a handcuff, and she didn't release it until all the guests had filed out of the parlor.

If I could ease through the crowd in the entry hall without Mr. or Mrs. Cahill spotting me, Fiona thought, I could get away clean.

And I could never face Pauline or Barbara or a bee again.

Fiona edged into the entry hall, keeping near the walls, trying to look as if she belonged there.

She slipped into the dining room.

Pauline and Barbara stood before the wedding cake.

Before Fiona could mention the bee, Pauline whispered, "I know! It was practically under my *nose* all through the wedding!"

Barbara looked at the long table. "If we could scrape the fillings off enough of those sandwiches and kind of plaster the cake with it—"

"It would taste like horseradish and pimientos," Fiona said.

Barbara held her hands up like an orchestra conductor. "Okay. Okay. If we could stick enough of the candy mints on the side, they wouldn't taste too odd."

"They'd look like cobblestones," Pauline said.

"Hey, it's your sister's dumb cake," Barbara snapped.

People began drifting into the dining room. Fiona had only to step out the French doors and make a dash for home . . . and leave the bee in the begonia in the bride's bouquet.

147

With Pauline and Barbara, she turned her back to the cake.

The bride and groom entered, surrounded by people.

Barely moving her lips, Fiona told Pauline, "Your sister still has her bouquet! You've got to warn her!"

"Warn her?" Pauline kept her back to the cake. "Warn her? She's already had a fit about the flowers and she hasn't even seen the cake. If I tell her she's holding a bee, I might as well throw a cherry bomb into the room."

Fiona kept her voice low. "Then you have to get those flowers away from her. You know how people are afraid of bees."

"You know how afraid *I* am of bees?" Pauline demanded.

The bride and groom came toward the cake table, followed by Mr. and Mrs. Cahill and the guests.

Fiona backed around the table and out the French doors, then stood to one side so she could see in without being noticed.

"Move, honey," Mr. Cahill told Pauline. "Your sister wants to cut the cake now. She's a little . . . tired."

Pauline stepped back.

"Pauline!" Mrs. Cahill grabbed her. "*You backed right into the cake! You've ruined it!*

Fiona stood frozen, astonished by Pauline's presence of mind.

Wielding her bouquet in both hands like a bat, the bride stepped forward.

Mrs. Cahill seized the bouquet.

Barbara shoved Pauline out the French doors.

With Fiona, they hurried around the side of the house to the back.

"That bee can't take any more racketing around," Fiona said. "You've got to tell your mother, Pauline."

"I don't dare go *near* her!" Pauline protested. "She and my father *paid* for this wedding. Besides, she's more scared of bees than I am."

"So imagine what will happen if that bee stings her," Fiona argued.

Barbara stopped by the back door. "You're the one who likes bees, Fiona. You have a way with bees. Bees take to you."

"It's not the bee that scares me so much as the people," Fiona said. "I'm not even supposed to be here. You expect me to just stroll in and take the bride's bouquet out of your mother's hands and walk away? One of you has got to get it."

"Snatch a bouquet with a bee in it?" Barbara asked. "Besides, if anybody tries to make off with it, she might as well confess that she knows how the bee got there."

The back door opened. "Pauline," Aunt Maytrue said, "your sister's leaving. She's . . . fatigued. The flower girls should be there when she throws her bouquet."

"That's no way to get rid of a bee!" Fiona cried, too

149

shocked to care what Aunt Maytrue thought.

"No!" Barbara clapped a hand to her forehead. "That's what a bride does just before she leaves the reception. She throws her bouquet into the crowd, *and everybody tries to catch it!*"

There was no time to worry about crashing the wedding. Dashing past Aunt Maytrue, Fiona raced through the kitchen and the dining room into the front hall.

Pauline's sister was halfway up the steps, leaning over the banister. Guests crowded around the foot of the staircase, laughing and yelling.

"Wait! Halt! Stop!" Fiona wriggled through the crush.

Nobody heard her in all the shrieks as the bride threw the bouquet.

Shoving in front of all the leaping, grabbing adults, Fiona jumped.

She had never jumped so hard, or so high, except in dreams.

As she felt her hand close around the stems, she ducked and then ran back through the dining room and the kitchen and out the door. Gently, she set the bouquet on a bush.

"Fiona Foster!" A hand fell on her shoulder and turned her around. Mrs. Cahill's voice trembled with fury. "That was the most outrageous, shocking, rude—"

"Mama!" Pauline cried. "There was a bee in the begonia in the bride's bouquet!"

*　　*　　*

Fiona went home and told her parents everything that had happened—before anybody else could.

She was sitting on her front porch in her old jeans when Pauline and Howard and Larry and Barbara came over with Spike, but without Oliver.

"My mother says she will never trust me to watch him again," Barbara said, "so the day wasn't all bad."

"Are your folks still upset?" Fiona asked Pauline.

"Mainly with Barbara and me for dumping Oliver on you. They said you were pretty brave to catch the bouquet."

"But they agree with my parents that you're a born troublemaker," Barbara put in.

Fiona scratched an old mosquito bite on her ankle. "My parents said I was asking for it, hanging around weddings where I'm not invited."

"Boy," Howard said in disgust. "Here you save everybody from a bee, and a panic, and nobody even says thanks. Who else would even try to catch a bouquet with a bee in it?"

"You should have seen her," Pauline told him. "Straight up in the air. Greatest catch I ever saw."

"You guys want to play ball?" Larry asked.

"If Fiona will catch," Barbara said.

"Sure," Howard agreed. "Who else?"

9

"Baseball," Fiona told her father a few weeks later, "is not all that great." She was on the floor of the family room, leaning against the sofa, wondering when one of her parents would tell her it was time to get ready for bed.

"I thought the team needed you." Her father looked around him on the sofa, then stood up and looked where he'd been sitting.

"They do." Fiona didn't ask what he was searching for, for fear he'd make her help. "But I've been playing for over a month, and I still can't see what makes it so terrific. There's more to life than standing around to catch a ball and throw it and try to hit it and, maybe once in a game, run."

Her mother looked up from the computer printout she was reading. "If you don't like it, why don't you quit?"

"Because they need me."

"Are you sitting on the *TV Guide* again?" Mr. Foster asked Mrs. Foster.

"I'd feel it if I were." She didn't bother getting up. "Fiona, all your life people are going to tell you that you *should* do what they *want* you to do. They'll tell you they'll be disappointed, or you'll ruin everything, if you don't. You can spend your life doing what other people want you to do, so that you never get around to doing what you want to do. You may even lose track of what it is."

"Fiona," Mr. Foster said, "stand up and see if you're sitting on the *TV Guide*."

Fiona stood up.

"Look at it this way," her mother said. "How much are they truly going to suffer if you don't play?"

"They'll lose even more games." Fiona sat down again.

"Then they'll have to find another good catcher. You didn't force them to play baseball." Mrs. Foster put the printout on the end table and held out her arms. I'm getting kind of big for this, Fiona thought, but she climbed into her mother's lap, anyway.

Mr. Foster looked under the sofa cushions. "Would you have left it upstairs?"

"Could you at least try to take an interest in your

153

child's problems?" Mrs. Foster asked him.

"I'll take an interest after I find out what's on TV," he said.

It's probably just as well, Fiona thought. If he gave me different advice, I'd have to sort it out.

Fiona played baseball with the team on Saturday. At the end of the game, after Howard had recovered the ball and Larry had examined his bat for cracks and Barbara had told everybody what they'd done wrong, Fiona said, "I'm not going to be playing anymore."

"What do you mean?" Howard demanded. "You can't just quit!"

"You don't have to take everything so *personally*," Barbara huffed.

"It's nothing you said," Fiona told her. "I just don't want to play anymore."

Pauline looked upset. "You have to play! It'll ruin everything if you don't!"

"Where would we get another catcher?" Larry asked.

They talked for another ten minutes, but everybody said the same thing over and over.

"I've got to get home," Fiona said finally.

She walked off the field, leaving the others arguing about what they were going to do for a catcher. At the chain link fence, Barbara caught up with her. "Why are you going to quit, really?"

"I don't much like baseball," Fiona confessed.

They walked along silently for a half a block. The

154

grass around the field had gone brown, and the air was hazy. The sun looked pale and feeble in the wintry sky.

Barbara scuffed along watching her shoes. Finally, she said, "I thought everybody liked baseball."

Fiona shrugged.

"Everybody's *supposed* to like baseball. I never heard anybody come right out and say she didn't. What will we do instead?"

Fiona stopped. *"We?"*

Barbara looked partly embarrassed and partly relieved. "I hate baseball. Standing around getting dust in your socks, and always afraid a ball's going to come and bend your fingers backward. That's the worst part. No—the worst part is being afraid you won't even try to catch the ball because you're so scared it will bend your fingers back."

It had never occurred to Fiona that Barbara was afraid of anything.

"You know what I'd really like to do after school?" Barbara mused. "I'd like to climb up in those tall trees by the library with a bunch of neat comic books to read."

"That would be nice," Fiona agreed, "unless it was raining."

The more she thought about reading comic books in the tall trees by the library, the better it sounded. Sunday she dug out all her comic books, so she and Barbara could trade while they read.

Monday after school she rushed to meet Barbara coming out of her class. "You want to go read comic books?"

"I have to play ball."

Fiona hurried to keep up with her. "You said you were going to quit."

"I told everybody I was, but they said that would ruin everything."

Fiona walked home alone and shoved all her comic books under the bed, knowing she'd just have to drag them all out again when her mother discovered them.

If Barbara could be talked out of quitting baseball, she thought, maybe the world was full of people who seemed tougher than they were.

Walking to school the next morning, Barbara was grumpier than Fiona had ever seen her. "I knew it would happen. I knew it. I tried to catch the ball, and it crashed into the ends of my fingers and bent them all backward. I don't know when I'll even be able to write my name again."

Neither Larry nor Howard nor Pauline had any answer for that. They all hung back, so Fiona was left walking beside Barbara.

Fiona knew better than to try to sympathize with her. "You want to go get our comic books after school and climb the trees?"

Barbara looked at her in astonishment. "With my fingers all bent back? The linaments are probably all stretched out."

"Ligaments," Fiona said.

"If I tried to get hold of a branch, I'd slip and *break* all my fingers. Anyway, it's probably against the law to climb the library trees. You can't have a bunch of kids in all the trees at the library."

In a few days it was too cold and drizzly to read in a tree anyway.

Barbara refused to play any more baseball. She said her linaments might get permanently stretched.

She spent more time with Fiona, but Fiona knew that was only because Pauline was still playing baseball.

10

The first week of December, Barbara started talking about her Christmas shopping. "I'm going to get Pauline some blue stationery and a pen with green ink. People never write in green on blue. They ought to. I'll get Howard a dog training book, if I can find a cheap one. Then for Larry, I thought about those stickers you put on yourself that look like real tattoos."

"You think his parents would let him look as if he's tattooed?"

"Fiona, you are basically a very dull person."

"Barbara, you are basically a grump," Fiona said firmly.

Barbara narrowed her eyes menacingly.

"A genuine grump," Fiona added.

Barbara tried to scowl, but the corners of her mouth twitched.

Fiona was surprised. Either she knows she's a grump and it doesn't bother her, she thought, or she knows and nobody ever came right out and told her before.

Barbara recovered herself before she broke down and actually smiled. "So," she asked, very, very casually, "do you want to go Christmas shopping together someday?"

On Saturday Fiona went to the market with her father, "I guess I should make out a Christmas list," she told him.

"Of what you want?" He picked two boxes of cereal off the bottom shelf.

"Of the people to give presents to."

"Whom do you have?"

"Just relatives, and then I don't know."

"That's a short list." He tossed two loaves of whole wheat bread into the cart.

"Barbara's giving presents to Pauline and Larry and Howard, and I don't know who else. I don't know if she's giving to me. I don't know if any of them are giving to me."

After Fiona's father paid for the groceries, he said, "Let's go get something to drink."

He took her to a place where the booths were upholstered in pink vinyl and the floor was big black and white squares.

After they ordered, he leaned forward, elbows on the table. "You don't want to wait to give presents until you know who's going to give them to you. You should give a gift because you want to, whether you expect anything back or not."

"If you give somebody a present and they don't have one for you, they'd be embarrassed, and then you'd be, too."

"This is true," he admitted.

"I don't think any of them are going to give me anything."

"Why?"

She shrugged. "Well, we're friends, and they even fought for my poster, but I still kind of feel like an outsider."

That week, Fiona made out her Christmas list. She thought a magazine rack would be good for her father, until she asked her mother what one would cost.

"Twenty, twenty-five dollars," Mrs. Foster said.

"That's out."

"With a little bit of glue and felt and sewing, you could make him a cover for the *TV Guide*."

"He'd put the *Guide* in it and then sit on the whole thing."

Saturday, Fiona's father took her shopping for a live Christmas tree. Maybe he wasn't perfect, she thought, but at least he would never kill a tree just for decoration.

The day was clear, and so cold the end of Fiona's

nose tingled. The Christmas-tree lot was like a strange, fantastic forest, with some of the trees flocked with fake snow, some dyed pink and blue. The smell, though, was all real—the sharp, dry, clean fragrance of live evergreens.

The other people moving through the lot would appear for a second through the trees and then disappear, like wood spirits.

As Fiona and her father wandered among the firs and pines and cypresses, looking for the live trees, she said, "My mother is not the kind of person who wears colored stockings."

He touched the needles of a short, spindly tree, almost as if to comfort it. "No, she's not."

"Still, I think I'll give her some purple ones. Then maybe you'll get invited to someplace exciting."

Fiona included Barbara, Pauline, Howard, Larry, even Spike and Oliver, on her shopping list. She could see her father's point. It's fun to give presents, even if you don't get any back, she realized.

On the other hand, she had fifteen dollars and sixty-two cents saved.

The first day of Christmas vacation Barbara came over, leading Oliver by the hand. He was wearing a red snowsuit with a hood, red mittens, and red boots, and he looked as if he'd been stuffed. "I've decided to give my sister a hamster for Christmas," Barbara announced, standing in the Fosters' entry hall. "Now that she's married, she misses our cat. My father would just as soon give her the cat, but Oliver and I would never forgive him. My sister's husband is allergic to cats, anyway."

"How do you know he's not allergic to hamsters?" Fiona was about to ask her and Oliver to take off their coats and snowsuits and boots and scarves and mittens and stay, but she decided there was no point in such an undertaking if they were all going to go out and play again.

Barbara chilled her with a glance. "Did you ever hear of anybody who was allergic to hamsters?"

"Why do you want to give her something that has to live in a cage?"

"You want her hamster wandering around her apartment, maybe getting trapped in the dishwasher or the sofa springs?"

Arguing with Barbara would only make her more determined to get a hamster, Fiona knew. Besides, it would be better off with Barbara's sister than living in some pet-shop window. A terrible thought struck Fiona. *What happened to leftover hamsters, the ones that didn't get bought*?

"Tell your mother we're going," Barbara prompted.

"Where?"

Barbara barely concealed her impatience. "To the pet shop. How can I hang on to Oliver and buy a hamster?" She unzipped the front of Oliver's snowsuit jacket and pushed back the hood. Already he looked flushed and sweaty.

Fiona wasn't that sure she wanted to risk going to a store with Barbara and her brother. She thought of the Lawson wedding, and the Cahill wedding, and Dr. Pollard's waiting room. "Which pet shop?"

"Right down on Twenty-fifth Avenue. You know my mother would never let me go downtown."

On the other hand, Fiona thought, it's kind of exciting to go Christmas shopping with somebody. "Molberry's has a pet department."

"Yeah, and it's in the mall. I'm not allowed to take Oliver that far."

As she got her coat and boots out of the hall closet, Fiona said, "I thought your parents were never going to let you watch him again."

"They have to. They're in the middle of Christmas shopping."

Fiona carried her coat into her mother's office. "Barbara wants me to go the pet shop on Twenty-fifth."

"Be back in an hour," Mrs. Foster said.

There was a fine, fine haze in the air, like a snowstorm that hadn't really got itself together. It was so cold, the few people on the street hurried along, heads down, their breath clouding in front of them. Oliver trotted between Barbara and Fiona, his arms raised, his mittened hands in theirs.

Twenty-fifth Avenue was a two-block strip of little

163

stores, none of them flashy, running through a neighborhood of small, middle-aged houses. The pet shop was sandwiched between an appliance-repair business and a beauty salon. In the window was a display of dog and cat beds and toys, and a sign that read RE-MEMBER YOUR BEST FRIEND THIS CHRISTMAS.

There were half a dozen customers in the pet shop, and two clerks with green smocks over their street clothes.

"Hang on to Oliver," Barbara told Fiona, "and keep him away from fish."

Oliver let Fiona take his hand. She was glad to see there were no puppies or kittens in the windows. As much as she would have loved to have had one, she hated to see them sold like nail polish or garden rakes.

On one side of the shop were fish in tanks. On the other were birds in cages. Fiona supposed people who bought birds liked them. But how could anybody who liked birds keep them from flying?

She steered Oliver over to a display of flea dips.

Barbara studied a cage with four hamsters in it.

At last a clerk noticed her. "You see one you want?"

"They're all brown," Barbara said. "Don't you have anything but plain brown?"

He looked a little insulted. "This close to Christmas, we're lucky to have any."

"Okay, give me a big one." Barbara pointed at the cage. "That one."

He plunged his hand into the cage and lifted out a hamster, which struggled for only a second and then gave up. How would it feel, Fiona wondered, to be suddenly snatched out of your world by an enormous hand?

"This one?" the clerk asked Barbara.

"I can't tell. You grabbed it too fast."

"If you can't tell, what does it matter?"

"Okay." She unzipped her purse.

"You'll need a cage," he said, "and a water bottle and a wheel."

"I know."

When they left the shop, Barbara carrying the hamster in its cage, Fiona asked, "Where did you get all that *money*?"

"My mother and father and grandparents all give me money to buy presents. And I saved my birthday money, and Oliver's."

"What did he buy?"

"Part of the cage."

"How will you gift wrap it without cutting off the air?"

Barbara looked at her and sighed. "I'm going to keep it in my room until my sister and her husband come over Christmas day. Then I'll just tie a red bow on the cage. That'll give me time to tame the hamster."

The next morning Barbara came over with the hamster in its cage and Oliver in his snowsuit. "It bit me," she said. "Let's go return it for one that doesn't bite."

Fiona tried to think of a good and true excuse for staying home.

"I only need you to hang on to Oliver," Barbara said. "You don't have to talk or anything."

Fiona went into her mother's office. "Barbara wants me to come with her to trade in the hamster she bought."

Her mother turned off the printer. "Trade in a hamster?"

"It bit her."

"Figures. All right, you may go, but then come right home."

There were even more customers in the pet shop than there'd been the day before.

"I'm sorry," the clerk told Barbara. "We're clean out of hamsters. You want to trade it for a nice rat?"

"Give my sister a rat for Christmas?" Barbara looked shocked.

He shrugged. "Rodents are rodents."

"What are rodents?" Barbara asked cautiously.

"Mice, rats, hamsters, squirrels . . ."

"Mice are out," she said.

"So are squirrels. We don't carry them."

Barbara left the store, followed by Fiona and Oliver.

"We'll have to trade in the hamster at Molberry's," Barbara said.

"But you didn't buy it there," Fiona reminded her.

"It's brand-new. And I'm sure not going to keep it."

Fiona could think of no answer. She doubted that animal shelters took hamsters. If they did, how could they find a good home for one that bit? Her own parents would never let her have it, especially since her mother knew it bit. The only chance for this hamster was to be bought by somebody who didn't like to handle rodents. But then who would clean its cage and fill its water bottle and feed it?

It's a hard world, Fiona thought, for any creatures people buy and sell.

"I didn't ask permission to go to the mall," she told Barbara. "And you're not suppose to take Oliver there."

"Look, you want me to give my sister a killer hamster?"

Fiona took off her coat and draped it over the cage to protect the hamster, who was very small, and alone, and about to be traded in. "That was a nice rat in the pet shop."

"You're covering up my arm," Barbara grumbled.

"Nice rat," Oliver said.

Barbara threw her arms out at her sides, cage and coat and all. "There. Okay. You did it. Are you satisfied? Now he's got four real words, 'Poor fish' and 'Nice rat.'"

Fiona had not forgotten that Barbara had never told her parents where Oliver had picked up "poor fish." Keeping quiet about where he got "nice rat" would be harder.

"Let's get to the mall," Barbara said. "The sooner

we finish this hamster business, the sooner Oliver will get rodents off his mind."

Feeling more or less responsible for Oliver's first real words, Fiona could hardly refuse. As soon as they reached Molberry's, she decided, she'd go to the optical department and ask her father to telephone her mother and get permission for her to be where she was.

The sidewalk around Molberry's was crowded with people admiring the Christmas scenes in the windows. Inside, the store was packed, noisy and festive, decorated with pink clouds and Styrofoam reindeer. On a glided throne on a platform by the menswear department, a live Santa Claus sat. Women dressed in brown leotards and tights with green jerkins and green knit caps were stationed around the ropes that set off the platform, herding the tots who clustered around into a single-file line.

"Oliver, will you pick up your feet?" Barbara snapped. "And will you take your coat off my arm and hang on to him, Fiona?"

"I already carried him the last block." Fiona took her coat and put it on. "While you exchange the hamster, I'll go explain to my father why we came without permission. If it takes you long, I'll bring Oliver down here to see Santa."

"I'm not supposed to let Oliver out of my sight. Besides, he can't stand Santa Claus. He's pretty violent about it."

Fiona was amazed. "About *Santa*?"

"Listen, if you could remember when you were Oliver's age and some fat guy in a fake white beard and wig and red suit plopped you on his lap and started bellowing, 'HO! HO! HO!' at you, I'll bet you weren't crazy about him, either. Oliver just isn't brainwashed yet."

Oliver gazed at Santa, his eyes narrowed.

"Uh-oh!" Handing the hamster cage to Fiona, Barbara steered Oliver away from the gilded throne.

"We'd better go see my father first." Fiona was feeling more and more uneasy.

"I'm not supposed to *be* here," Barbara protested.

"If we don't go see him, and somebody tells him we're here when we don't have permission . . ."

"Let me get rid of the hamster first." Barbara boosted Oliver, who was craning around to glare at Santa, onto the UP escalator.

The second floor was as crowded as the first, with Christmas carols booming from the loudspeakers.

At the pet department, Fiona handed the cage to Barbara and hung back, holding Oliver's hand. There was no need to let the whole world know she was with Barbara.

Making her way past the shoppers, Barbara approached a clerk who was coming out of the stockroom with her arms full of cat Christmas stockings. "I want to trade in this hamster."

The clerk seemed taken aback. *"Trade in a hamster? For what?"*

"A hamster," Barbara said patiently. "This one bit me."

"If it bit you, you must have handled it wrong." The clerk set the stockings on the counter and opened the hamster cage. Reaching in, she lifted out the hamster. "There's nothing wrong with this animal."

"If I'd had to have had stitches," Barbara said, "my mother probably would have sued somebody."

The clerk looked down at her for a second. "You just want to trade in the hamster."

"Sure. The cage is okay."

"All right." She led Barbara to a cage with half a dozen hamsters in it. "Pick one."

Barbara pointed at a hamster. "That one looks harmless."

The clerk put Barbara's hamster in the store cage. She took out the one Barbara had selected and put it in Barbara's cage. "Don't go grabbing at it, or picking it up when it wants to be left alone."

"Thank you," Barbara said. "Where's the bathroom?"

"That was easy," she told Fiona as they left the pet department. "Now we just have to be sure this one doesn't bite before I take it home."

"It didn't bite the clerk," Fiona pointed out.

Barbara was firm. "Neither did the one that bit me."

She led Fiona and Oliver across the store, through the teeming aisles, to the women's lounge.

Fiona stopped. "We can't take Oliver in there!" she protested.

"We're taking a hamster, aren't we?"

"I don't think we're supposed to do that either.'"

"You see a 'No Hamsters' sign anywhere? We just keep Oliver in the part where the mirrors and sofas are." Shoving open the door, Barbara walked in.

Oliver lurched after her.

Since she was holding his hand, Fiona went with him. She couldn't make a scene scuffling with a toddler outside the women's lounge in the store where her father worked—especially when she was in the store without permission.

To her relief, she and Barbara and Oliver were the only people in the first section of the lounge.

It was separated from the bathroom part by a partition that reached from the floor almost to the ceiling, and it was an altogether elegant place—especially for an area that led to a bathroom. On one wall was a huge mirror in a gilded frame. A curved-back sofa with red, velvety upholstery and tall, gilded legs was flanked by two end tables with the same high, curved legs and tops that looked a lot like inlaid wood. At right angles to the sofa were two chairs with gilded frames and satin upholstery in wide pale-blue and gold stripes.

Sitting on the beige carpet, Barbara opened the cage door.

"I don't think—" Fiona began.

The hamster shot out of the cage. Startled, Barbara

jerked back. Then she grabbed for him, but he scurried under the sofa. "Oh, rats!" she groaned.

"Nice rat!" Oliver flopped onto his stomach to peer after it.

On the other side of the partition that separated the two sections of the lounge, a toilet flushed.

"Don't just stand there! Help me get it!" Dropping to her hands and knees, Barbara looked under the sofa.

Fiona heard a faucet turned on. She slid under the sofa after the hamster—it seemed like a good place to avoid being identified.

She heard footsteps coming from the other half of the lounge. Then she saw a pair of high-heeled boots.

"Nice rat!" Oliver called.

The hamster scurried from under the sofa.

The boots scuttled out of the lounge.

"There it is again!" As Barbara dived for the hamster, it ran along the baseboards, around the partition, into the bathroom section.

The door from the sales floor opened, and Fiona saw four shoes enter.

"Nice rat!" Oliver called again.

"Get him out of here!" Barbara ran after the hamster.

The shoes turned and rushed out of the lounge.

Careful not to hit her head, Fiona backed out from under the sofa.

She stood up and looked around her.

There was no sign of Oliver.

"Is Oliver in there with you?" she called.

"He's out there with you," Barbara yelled from the other section of the lounge.

Fiona ran out onto the sales floor.

The aisles were thronged with shoppers. "Oliver!" Fiona shouted, but her voice was lost in "Silent Night" coming from the loudspeakers.

Fiona shoved and wriggled through the crowd. She looked under and around the beds in the Sleep Shop. She riffled through the hanging draperies in Window Coverings. She looked behind the rug samples in Floor Coverings.

"Silent Night" ended, and "Hark, the Herald Angels Sing," and "Rudolph, the Red-Nosed Reindeer," and Fiona had worked her way to Toyland.

The centers of the aisles were thronged, but every few seconds she could glimpse something besides backs and bags and packages. A few feet ahead of her a woman took a cap gun away from a little girl and set it firmly on the counter. "No. No guns this Christmas, or any Christmas."

As the woman led the girl away, a very small boy reached up and took the gun off the counter.

"Oliver!" Fiona cried.

Her voice was drowned out by a man's jovial announcement over the loudspeaker: "Kids! Santa Claus is downstairs on our main-floor Christmasland! *Don't miss Santa!*"

173

Fiona tried to squeeze through to where she had glimpsed Oliver.

"Hurry, kids!" urged the voice from the loud-speaker. "This may be your last shot at Santa!"

Jostled and buffeted, Fiona managed to reach the spot where she'd seen Oliver.

He was gone.

11

With her heart thudding like a drum in her head, Fiona threaded her way through the crush, glancing desperately around her.

She did not see Oliver on the escalators. Not only was he at large in the store, cap gun in hand, but a loudspeaker was urging him to take a shot at Santa.

Fiona turned, weaving her way through the crowd back to the women's lounge.

Barbara squatted on the floor, shutting the door of the hamster cage. "He didn't even try to bite. Scared a few people who came in, but they didn't stay." She looked up, "Where's Oliver?"

"He shoplifted a cap gun and got away in the toy department," Fiona said hoarsely.

Barbara stood, looking pale and terrified. Fiona opened the door. Without a word Barbara followed her out of the lounge.

Fiona led the way, with Barbara so close the hamster cage nudged Fiona's back.

At the toy department, Barbara handed Fiona the cage and stood up on a wagon to look around.

The voice from the loudspeaker was so sudden, so loud, that Fiona reached up to steady Barbara. "Kids! Santa is on our main floor! Be sure not to miss Santa! This may be your last shot!"

Barbara stepped off the wagon. "You say Oliver's running loose with a *cap gun*?"

Fiona nodded. "We can't search this whole store. The only thing is to get my father to have them broadcast his description and order him not to move."

"There's no time! He may be headed for Santa right now!" Barbara shoved Fiona through the crowd toward the escalators.

As they stepped on the DOWN escalator, Fiona looked over its rail. She could see all the way over the crowds to Santa on his throne.

Oliver was third in a line of tots waiting to talk to him.

"No, Oliver!" Barbara yelled over the rail. "Oliver, don't do it!"

People on the steps below them turned around. People passing on the UP escalator stared.

"He can't hear you," Fiona said before Barbara could yell again.

There was no way around the people on the steps below. Fiona could only stand and try in her mind to hurry the escalator.

"Don't look down," she advised Barbara, but she couldn't help looking herself.

A girl got off Santa's lap and a boy climbed on. Oliver was next in line.

"He's going to do it," Barbara moaned. "I know he's going to do it. And I'll get the blame. They'll send me to a boarding school where you have to wear knee socks all year round."

The instant she and Fiona reached the bottom of the escalator, they leaped off and pushed through the aisle, heading for Christmasland.

Near Santa's platform they split up, each racing along one side of the line.

"No crowding in!" One of the women in leotards and tights grabbed for Fiona.

Fiona ducked out of her grasp.

The boy on Santa's lap slid off, and Oliver stepped forward. He held the gun down at his side, his finger on the trigger.

"Oliver!" Barbara yelled. "Freeze!"

As Barbara tackled him, Fiona seized his gun arm.

The elf dragged Oliver and Barbara to their feet and glared down at them. "You! Out!"

Oliver looked at the cap gun in Fiona's hand. "Oh, rats," he said.

Fiona headed for the UP escalator.

Holding the cage in one hand and Oliver by the other, Barbara caught up with her. "What are you doing? They ordered us out!"

Fiona didn't break her stride. "We are going to turn ourselves in."

Barbara stared at her, astonished. "You're out of your mind!"

"To my father. The store detectives could be on our trail right now, and I am holding a shoplifted cap gun that came *that* close to ruining Santa's whole season."

They rode up the escalator, Barbara holding Oliver's arm.

Two women on the step above turned to smile down at him.

"Look at that face," one said. "Is that an angel face or is that an angel face?"

"Have you seen Santa yet, sweetheart?" the other asked him.

Barbara tightened her grip on Oliver's arm.

There was not a customer in the optical department. Mr. Foster was arranging tinted plastic lenses on a velvet-lined tray. He smiled at Barbara and Fiona and Oliver. "What are you doing here? Who's with you?"

"Just us." Fiona held the gun out. "Oliver kind of . . . picked this up. Could you get it back to the toy department?"

Her father took the gun. "How can you expect to raise sane, law-abiding citizens when every kid packs a gun? The store shouldn't even carry the miserable things."

"It certainly should not," Barbara said fervently.

"I'm going to eat in a few minutes," he said. "You can call your mothers, and if it's all right, I'll treat you to lunch in the coffee shop."

"The thing is," Fiona said carefully, "we don't have specific permission to be here."

"Not *specific*," Barbara agreed. "On the other hand, my mother didn't tell me specifically not to come to Molberry's today."

Instead of treating them to lunch, Mr. Foster called their mothers and then drove them directly home.

Nobody spoke in the car.

Finally, as if he felt somebody ought to make conversation, Oliver leaned toward Mr. Foster. "Nice rat."

Mrs. Lawson was waiting in front of her house. "You," she greeted Barbara. "Straight to your room."

It was three days before Fiona dared try to converse with her mother. "There is something about Barbara that just tends to get me in trouble," she said then. "I mean, how many people do you know who get grounded for three days in the week before Christmas?"

"Two," Mrs. Foster said. "Barbara also has sensible parents."

On December twenty-second, Barbara came over without Oliver. She carried the hamster in its cage, and a large grocery sack. Fiona wasn't sure whether she should ask permission to let a rodent into the house, but she couldn't leave him out in the cold. Nor could she leave Barbara standing on the porch with a bag that just might contain a Christmas present.

She led Barbara up to her room, hoping her mother would stay in her office.

"Boy." Barbara set the cage on Fiona's bed. "I don't know how you always manage to get me in trouble. I was grounded—"

"I know."

"Three days?"

Fiona nodded. "This is the first day they've even let me answer the door."

Barbara looked sober. "When parents start getting together like that, there's no telling where it will end. My folks even invited yours to their New Year's party."

"You're kidding!" Fiona was astonished.

"With any luck, they won't get to be *good* friends." Barbara set the sack on the bed. "I have to get back. I just came to deliver your present."

It was the most exciting thing that had happened to Fiona in three days. "Is it okay to look?"

Barbara seemed surprised. "Sure."

Fiona opened the sack. In it was a half-empty bag of hamster litter, and another of hamster food. "Oh." Fiona had never heard of anybody refusing a Christmas present. But there was something far more important than manners involved here.

She closed the sack. "Barbara, thank you for bringing me this, but I'm not going to get a hamster. I would never buy anything I'd have to keep in a cage. As a matter of fact, the more I think about it, the more it makes me mad the way you go out and buy animals and dump them and drag them around as if they were Barbie dolls or something. Just because they can't talk, or read or write, doesn't mean they don't hurt and get scared and sad as much as you do."

With a sigh Barbara picked up the cage and held it out to her. "Merry Christmas, dummy."

Fiona was too astounded to take it. "I thought you were going to give the hamster to your sister."

"I already did."

Fiona drew back. "It didn't . . ."

"Nah. It hasn't even tried to bite *me*. It just drove her and her husband crazy running around and around in that wheel all night. That's why I gave it to them early." She shrugged. "That's why they gave it back. Now my parents want it out of the house. They're upset about Oliver talking to it all the time."

"He still says—"

"All the time."

The hamster licked his paws and washed his face.

"Who else have you tried to give him to?" Fiona asked cautiously.

181

"After all you and I went through together?" Barbara looked hurt. "Besides, I'd trust you with an animal more than any kid I know." She set the cage on Fiona's desk.

"You're right," Fiona said. "Only, my parents are never going to let me keep a rodent." She looked at the hamster, who was gazing around him all cheerful and innocent, with no idea how many times he'd been rejected. "*Ordinarily* they would never let me keep a rodent. But it's three days before Christmas. They grounded me for three whole days. They've just made friends with your parents. How can they go to your folks' New Year's party if they make me give back your present?"

Barbara regarded her solemnly. "You know, you think more and better than most people, Fiona."

After Barbara left, Fiona sat on her bed and gazed at the hamster. "She likes me," she told him. "In her own grumpy way, Barbara really likes me. Only how did I end up with a pet that lives in a cage? That part just doesn't figure."

She waited until it was too late to call Barbara back. Then she strolled into her mother's office. "Barbara brought me a Christmas present."

Mrs. Foster looked up from the monitor. "That's nice."

Fiona nodded. "Especially since she was grounded for three shopping days the week before Christmas.

It's amazing that she has any Christmas spirit left."

Mrs. Foster let her fingers slide off the keyboard.

"It would really hurt her feelings if you made me give it back."

"Fiona, we'd never do a thing like that. Bygones are bygones. What you did is over, you've both spent three days grounded, and that's the end of it."

"I'm glad you feel that way."

Mrs. Foster turned her head slightly. "What is that squeaking in your room?"

"An exercise wheel."

Mrs. Foster got up and hurried to Fiona's room.

Fiona followed. "Look at it this way. It could have been a snake."

When Mr. Foster got home, he came in to look at the hamster. Then he and Fiona's mother went to their room and shut the door.

At last they came back to Fiona's room, looking solemn.

"You'll have to keep it strictly in your room," her mother said.

"That's what I wanted to talk about," Fiona said. "So if I keep my door closed and my eyes open, the hamster can run around in my room."

"Only when you're in there," her mother told her firmly. "I don't want it skittering all over the house."

"Neither do I!" Fiona said, remembering the women's lounge at Molberry's.

"You'll have to learn about hamster care." Mr. Foster was stern. "You have to feed it properly and keep its water fresh and the cage clean."

"I will," Fiona assured him.

"I'm still not crazy about the idea," her father said.

"It's cheaper than a dog," she reminded him.

After dinner that evening, Barbara telephoned her. "You want to come over the day after my folks' party? They said we can have the leftovers."

"Wow. Neat!" Stuffed mushrooms, Fiona thought. I *bet* they'll have stuffed mushrooms and barbecue-flavor almonds.

"Shall we ask Pauline and Larry and Howard?" Barbara asked. "It might be more fun with just the two of us."

"If somebody had a leftover party and didn't invite me, I'd feel bad. If it's a big party, there'll be plenty of leftovers. Do you suppose they'll have horns and party hats, too?"

"I don't know. I'd feel kind of dumb putting on a stupid hat and blowing horns the day after New Year's."

Fiona could see her point.

"You want to know what Pauline's giving you for Christmas?" Barbara asked.

"*No*." Fiona said.

"How about what Howard and Larry got for you?"

"Barbara, I don't want to know, so just drop it."

Barbara was silent for a moment, then, "I suppose

they didn't happen to mention to you what they were giving me?"

"They didn't, and I wouldn't tell you anyway."

Fiona lay awake that night listening to the hamster running in his wheel. She was beginning to see why he was so willing to be put back in his cage at bedtime.

Two days. Two days to get Christmas presents for everybody, she thought. I wonder if there's any felt and glue lying around the house.

Of course, now that I have a hamster, I don't need a dog dish. It's barely used. But it's probably too big for Barbara's cat. Besides, a Christmas present ought to be new.

On the other hand, this hamster has gone through two homes already.

I'll figure something out. If I can talk my parents into letting me keep a rodent in my room, I can talk them into an advance on my next few weeks' allowance. I'll ask for four weeks to start. If it hadn't been for me, they'd never be going to the Lawsons' New Year's party. They're probably going to start being invited to weddings and everything. All in all, it's going to be a pretty good Christmas.

Lulled by the steady squeaking of the hamster wheel, she drifted into sleep.